P9-DFQ-732

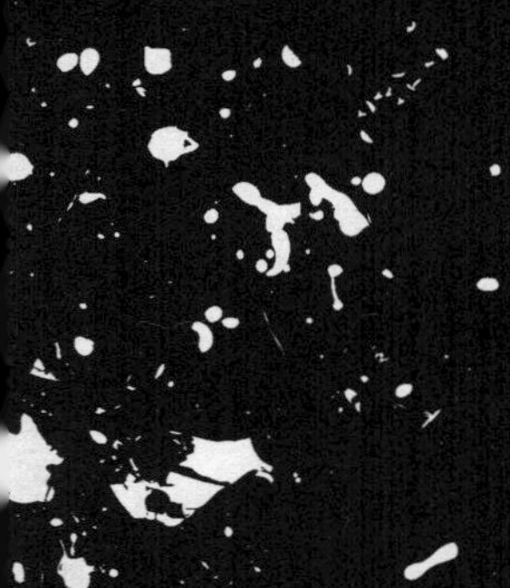

ZOM-B

UNDERGROUND

DARREN SHAN

ZOM-B

UNDERGROUND

LB LITTLE, BROWN AND COMPANY NEW YORK BOSTON

Little, Brown and Company

Hachette Book Group
237 Park Avenue, New York, NY 10017
Visit our website at www.lb-teens.com

Little, Brown and Company is a division of Hachette Book Group, Inc.
The Little, Brown name and logo are trademarks of Hachette Book Group, Inc.

The publisher is not responsible for websites (or their content) that are not owned by the publisher.

First Edition: January 2013
ISBN 978-0-316-21412-4

10 9 8 7 6 5 4 3 2 1

RRD-C

Printed in the United States of America

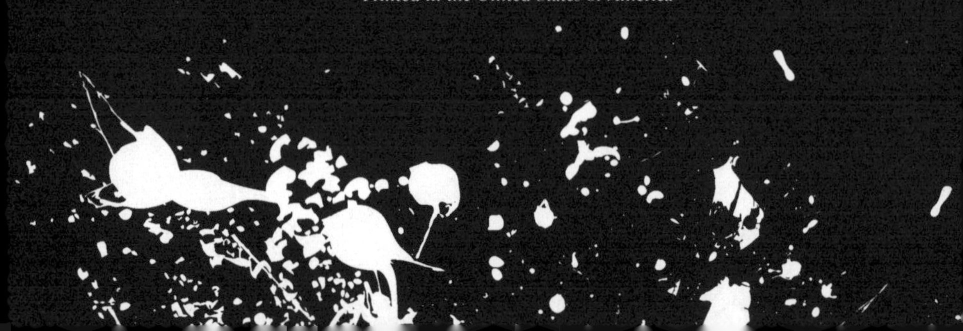

OBE (Order of the Bloody Entrails) to:
Kathryn "spielberg" McKenna

Edited in an underground complex by
Venetia Gosling
Kate Sullivan

Mr. Dowling is available for birthday parties and is
represented by:
The Christopher Little Agency

ALSO BY

DARREN SHAN

THE THIN EXECUTIONER

ZOM-B SERIES

ZOM-B

THE SAGA OF LARTEN CREPSLEY

BIRTH OF A KILLER

OCEAN OF BLOOD

PALACE OF THE DAMNED

BROTHERS TO THE DEATH

THE DEMONATA SERIES

LORD LOSS

DEMON THIEF

SLAWTER

BEC

BLOOD BEAST

DEMON APOCALYPSE

DEATH'S SHADOW

WOLF ISLAND

DARK CALLING

HELL'S HEROES

The Cirque Du Freak Series

A LIVING NIGHTMARE

THE VAMPIRE'S ASSISTANT

TUNNELS OF BLOOD

VAMPIRE MOUNTAIN

TRIALS OF DEATH

THE VAMPIRE PRINCE

HUNTERS OF THE DUSK

ALLIES OF THE NIGHT

KILLERS OF THE DAWN

THE LAKE OF SOULS

LORD OF THE SHADOWS

SONS OF DESTINY

THEN...

Becky Smith's father was a bully and a racist. He often beat B and her mum, when he wasn't working hard to stop the flow of immigrants into the country. B loved and feared him equally. She swore to herself that she didn't share his vicious, racist tendencies, but at the same time she never challenged him about them.

One of B's teachers, Mr. Burke, warned her that she risked becoming just like her dad if she continued to play along with him. But B had never paid much attention to what teachers said.

B was a tomboy and could hold her own with any guy her age. She liked music, surfing the Web, hanging out with her mates. Just an average girl who thought she'd lead a normal life and never do anything special.

Then zombies attacked her school. B and her friends didn't know how the dead had come back to life, or why so many of them were on the loose, or what the strange mutants who could control them were. And there was no time to find out. They had to run or die. So they ran.

B's dad rescued her. He led the group to safety, playing the part of a hero to perfection. Until they hit a snag and zombies closed in on them. To delay the zombies, he told B to throw a black boy named Tyler Bayor to them. And because she had always obeyed her father when he gave her a command, she did. The zombies bit into the screaming Tyler with relish as he begged B to save him.

Horrified by what she'd done, B abandoned her monstrous dad and raced back into the school, to search for another way out. But she only found zombies and mutants. Or rather, they found her.

On a staircase, the freshly zombified Tyler caught up with B. She had been scratched by another member of the undead and was terrified that she was about to turn into one of them. But Tyler took her mind off that worry when he ripped her chest open. The last thing she saw was Tyler biting into her still-beating heart.

Then she died.

ONE

NOW...

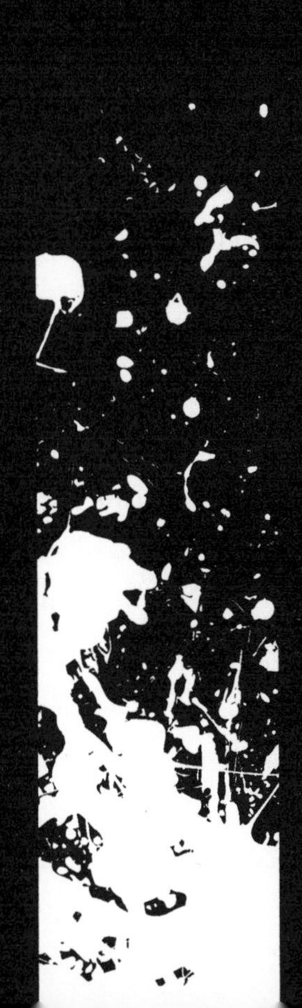

I smell burning hair. It's a nasty, acidic smell. I burned my eyebrows once when I was playing with a lighter and I've never forgotten that foul aroma. As my face wrinkles with distaste, an even nastier stench kicks in and I almost gag. What the hell *is* that?

As I'm trying to place the sickening scent, a tall man staggers past, face and skull ablaze, trying to slap out the flames but failing. He falls to his knees and shakes his head wildly from side to side, the flames growing thicker, glowing more brightly. And I peg the source of the smell.

It's burning flesh.

With a startled cry, I flail away from

the man on fire and glance around desperately for something to quench the flames with, or someone to call for help. It takes all of two seconds to realize I'm in just as much trouble as the guy with the burning pumpkin for a head.

I'm in a large room. Not one I recognize. I should be in my school, but this is a place I've never seen before. Pure white walls, except where they've been scorched. Several oversized windows, lots of people on the other side of the glass, peering in, studying the chaos.

There's a small team at the center of the room, six people in black leather pants and jackets, faces hidden behind the visors of motorcycle-type helmets. Each is armed, a couple with flame-throwers, another pair with stun guns, two with spears.

Lots of figures surround the six in leathers. Fifteen or so men, a handful of women, a couple of teenagers, a girl no more than eight or nine years old. Except they're not normal people. They're zombies.

I categorize them even before the memories of what happened at my school click into place. I've seen enough horror films to know a fully paid-up member of the living dead when I see one. They don't move as stiffly as most movie zombies, but they have the vacant expression, they're missing body parts, some are caked in blood, their teeth are gnashing together hungrily, they're covered in scars and cuts, and wisps of green moss grow over their wounds.

Wait...I never saw moss in any of the movies. I only saw that on the zombies in the Internet clips of the attack in Pallaskenry.

And on those who struck when my school was attacked. When *I* was killed.

I flash on a memory of Tyler Bayor jamming his hand into my chest and ripping out my heart. I moan pitifully and my hands snake to my breast to find out if that really happened or if it was just a dream. But I'm distracted before I can check.

One of the leather-clad tormentors at the center of the room is bigger than the others, tall and burly. He breaks away from the group and sprays flames in a wide semicircle, scorching the zombies closest to him. They squeal and peel away. It seems like the dead can feel pain too.

"Rage!" one of the others barks. "Get your arse back here. We've got to stick together."

"Sod that," the tall one retorts, and pushes forward, coming towards me, letting fly with more flames.

I forget about everything else and flee from the fire, survival instincts kicking in, following a man and woman who were singed from the last burst. I try to call to the guy in the leathers, to plead with him to stop, but there's something wrong with my mouth. It feels like it's full of pebbles. All that emerges is a strangled "*Urrggghh! Ugga gurhk!*" sound.

One of the zombies–a woman–leaps onto the tall guy's back and gnaws at his shoulder. He lowers his flamethrower, grabs her hair and tugs. She claws at his helmet. He bends over to shake her off.

While I'm not naturally inclined to side with a zombie, it's clear

that we're in the same boat. An enemy of theirs is also an enemy of mine. So I dart forward to help the undead woman tackle our foe with the flamethrower.

One of the others in the center yells a warning to the suitably named Rage, but it's too late. I rush him from his blind side and throw myself at him. I probably wouldn't be able to knock him over by myself, but the weight of the woman helps drag him down.

As the guy in the helmet yelps, I grab the hose of his flamethrower and wrestle it from him. He hangs on tightly, roaring for help, but then the woman bites his arm and digs through the leather of his jacket. With a curse, his grip loosens. A second later I've ripped the hose from the tanks strapped to his back and the device is rendered useless.

The person with the other flamethrower peels away from the group and starts towards me.

"Cathy!" someone shouts. "Don't break rank!"

"But Rage needs–"

"Forget about him. We need you to cover the rest of us."

As the woman hesitates, I heft the hose–it feels quite solid–and move in on the guy on the ground. He's pushing the female zombie away, trying to make room to kick at her. I take a couple of practice swings, then let him have it, bringing it down as hard as I can over the top of his helmet.

The guy bellows with pain and backs away from me as I swing at him again. The zombie gurgles and shoves me aside, hurrying after him, clawing at his legs like a cat as she tries to grab hold. My gaze fixes on the small bits of bone sticking out of the ends of her fingers and I'm stopped in my tracks by another flashback.

I glance down at my own hand and see bones jutting out of my fingers too. I drop the hose and clutch the hand to my chest, moaning softly. I check the other fingers and find more extended bones. I raise my head and shriek at the ceiling, a wordless cry of frustration and terror.

The guy on the floor lashes out with a foot and connects with the zombie's head. She's driven back. He forces himself to his feet and staggers towards the safety of his pack. Other zombies throw themselves in his path, clutch at him, gnash at his gloved fingers. But he's strong and moving fast. He brushes them aside as if they were mannequins, then slips behind the woman with the flamethrower and picks at the material around the place where the zombie bit him, examining his wound.

I chuckle sickly at the sight of the guy studying his arm. The bite of a zombie is contagious. He's finished. Any minute now he'll turn into one of them, and good riddance to the bugger. I've no sympathy for anyone who tries to burn me alive.

I look at my fingers again and the chuckle dies away at the back of my throat as I'm forced to correct myself. He'll turn into one of *us*.

A siren blares and panels slide open in the ceiling. As I stare, bewildered, nets drop through the gaps and fall on several of the zombies. There must be weights attached to the nets, because the zombies stagger, then fall. They become entangled as they writhe on the floor and are quickly trapped.

More nets drop and the rest of the zombies are swiftly subdued. They hiss and roar defiantly, and some try to flee, but the nets find them all, even the little girl. Soon I'm the only one left standing. For some reason they haven't targeted me. I squint at the ceiling as the panels are replaced, waiting for the area above me to open, but I'm either standing in a spot where they can't get at me or for some reason they don't want to ensnare me.

"Do you think I should toast this one?" the woman with the flamethrower asks, advancing past the struggling zombies.

I snarl at her and try to shout a curse, but again all that comes out is a gargled noise, something along the lines of "*Fwah ooo!*"

"Hold on," somebody says, and a guy with a spear puts it down, then removes his helmet. I stare uncertainly. It's a boy, my sort of age, maybe a bit younger. The rest start to take off their helmets and I'm astonished to find that all of them are teenagers. I look for a familiar face, but they're all strangers to me.

As four of the boys drop their helmets and study me with dark, suspicious expressions, the girl called Cathy takes off hers. She's scowling. She points the nozzle of her flamethrower at me again.

"She attacked Rage," Cathy growls. "I say we finish her off."

"They don't want us to," one of the boys mutters, nodding at the ceiling, then pointing at a window, where the people on the other side of the glass are watching calmly.

"All the more reason to burn her," Cathy sneers.

"Hold it!" the tall one–Rage–barks. He's still wearing his helmet. He strides over to the girl with the flamethrower and stares at her through the dark lens of his visor. "Nobody breaks the rules around here."

"But she attacked you," Cathy pouts. "She tried to kill you."

"Yeah," Rage says. "You would have too in her position. She's a zom head. We have to hand her over."

"She might not be," Cathy says. She still hasn't lowered the flamethrower.

Rage tilts his head, then looks back at me. "Got anything to say for yourself?"

Unable to express myself with words, I give him the finger.

Rage chuckles drily, then takes off his helmet. He's got a big head, hair cut even shorter than mine, chubby cheeks–a chunk of flesh has been bitten out of the left cheek and a layer of green moss grows lightly around it–small ears, beady eyes. He's grinning wickedly.

"Whaddaya know," he jeers, reaching out and bending my finger down. *"It's aliiiiive!"*

As I stare at him, more confused than I've ever been, a door swishes open. Soldiers and medics spill into the room and fan out around us.

The madness begins.

TWO

I'm B Smith and I'm a zombie.

I study my face in the small mirror in my cell, looking for a monster but only finding myself. I look much the same as I did before I was killed, hair shaved tight, pale skin, a few freckles, a mole on the far right of my jaw, light blue eyes, a nose that's a bit too wide for my face. But if I stare long enough I start to notice subtle differences.

Like those blue eyes I was always so pleased about. (I was never a girlie girl, but they were my best feature and, yeah, I used to admire them every so often if I was feeling gooey.) They're not as shiny as they were. They look like they've dried out. That's because they have.

I tilt my head back and pour several

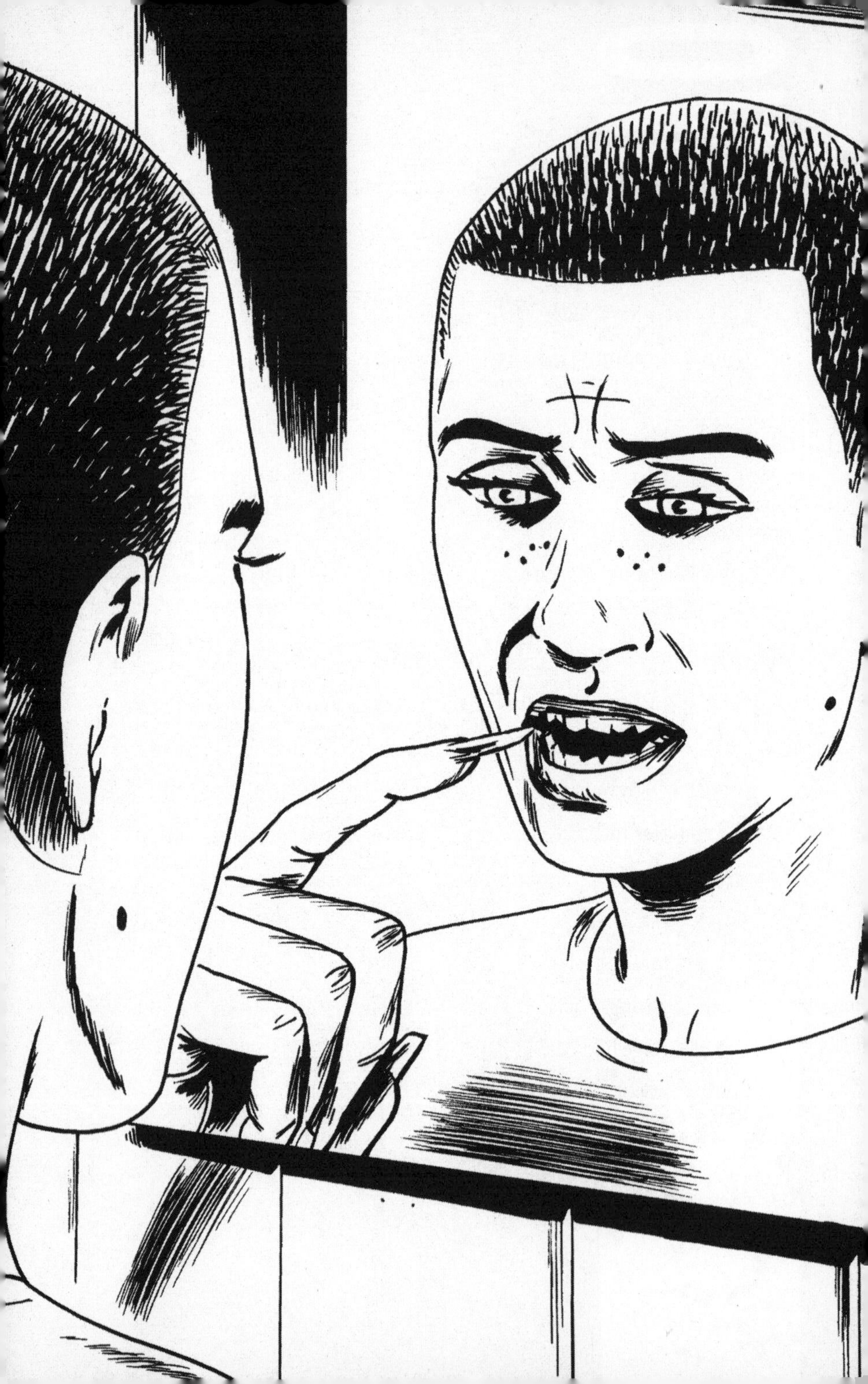

drops from a bottle into each eye, then shake my head gently from side to side to work the liquid about. Reilly gave me the bottle. He also taught me how to shake my head the right way.

"You can't blink anymore."

That was several days ago, not long after I was brought to my cell from the room of fire. I was bundled in here without anyone saying anything, no explanations, no sympathy, no warnings. After the horror show with the zombies and the gang in leather, a group of soldiers simply shuffled me along a series of corridors, stuck me here and left me alone.

For a few hours I paced around the small cell. There was nothing in it then, no mirror, no bed, no bucket. Just a sink that didn't have running water. I was wild with questions, theories, nightmarish speculations. I knew that I'd been killed and come back to life as a zombie. But why had my thoughts returned? Why could I remember my past? Why was I able to reason?

The zombies in Pallaskenry and my school were mindless, murdering wrecks. They killed because they couldn't control their unnatural hunger for brains. The zombies in the room were the same, single-minded killing machines on legs.

Except I thought that those teenagers with the weapons were zombies too. Rage had definitely been bitten by one of the undead—the moss growing around his cheek was proof of that. But they could talk and think and act the same way they could when they were alive.

What the hell was going on?

Reilly was the first person to enter my cell that day. A thickset soldier with brown hair and permanent stubble, he brought in a chair, closed the door behind him, put the chair in front of me and sat.

"You can't blink anymore," he said.

"*Uh urh ooh?*" I grunted, forgetting that I couldn't speak.

"You can't talk either," he noted drily. "We'll sort out your mouth soon but you should tend to your eyes first. Your vision will have suffered already, but the more they dry out, the worse it'll get."

He produced a plastic bottle of eye drops and passed it to me. As I stared at it suspiciously, he chuckled. "It's not a trick. If we wanted to harm you, we'd have fried you in the lab. Your eyelids don't work. Go on, try them, see for yourself."

I tried to close my eyes but nothing happened. If I furrowed my brow it forced them partly closed into a squint, but they wouldn't move by themselves. I reached for them to pull the lids down. Then I saw the bones sticking out of my fingers and stopped, afraid I might scratch my eyeballs.

"Good call," Reilly said. "Revitalizeds all come close to poking out an eye—a few actually did before we could warn them. Most reviveds instinctively know to keep their hands away from their eyes, but you guys..." He snorted, then told me how to administer the drops.

I stare at myself in the mirror again and wipe streaks from the drops away as they drip down my cheeks—the closest I'm ever going to get to tears now that I'm dead. My eyes look better, but still not as moist and sharp as they once did. I can see clearly, but my field of vision is narrower and the world's a bit darker than when I was alive, as if I'm staring through a thin gray veil.

I open my mouth and examine my teeth. Run a tongue over them, but carefully. I nicked it loads of times the first few days and I still catch myself occasionally.

After Reilly had given me the drops, he told me why I couldn't talk.

"Your teeth have sprouted. When you returned from the dead, they thickened and lengthened into fangs. That's so you can bite through flesh and bone more easily." He said it casually, as if it were no big thing.

"The bones in your fingers serve the same purpose," he went on. "They let you dig through a person's skull. Better than daggers, they are. We're not sure why it happens in your toes as well. Maybe the zombie gene can't distinguish between one set of digits and the other."

I wanted to cry when he said that. I don't know why, but something about his tone tore a long, deep hole through my soul. I made a moaning noise and hung my head, but no tears came. They couldn't. My tear ducts have dried up. I can never weep again.

Reilly went on to explain how they were going to file my teeth down. They'd use an electric file to start me off, but after that I could trim them with a metal file myself every day or two.

"It'll be like brushing your teeth," he said cheerfully. "A few minutes in the morning, again at night before you go to bed, and they'll be fine." He paused. "Although you won't really need to go to bed now. . . ."

It's been hard keeping track of the days, but by totaling up Reilly's visits I figure I've been here at least a week, maybe longer. And not a wink of sleep in all that time. They gave me a bed, and I lie down every now and then to rest, but I never come close to dropping off.

"The dead don't sleep," Reilly shrugged when I asked him why I couldn't doze. "They don't need to."

I was nervous when a medic first filed my teeth down. I always hated going to the dentist, and this was a hundred times worse. The noise was louder than any dentist's drill, and splinters from my teeth went flying back in my throat and up my nose and into my eyes. My teeth got hot from the friction and my gums felt like they were burning. I pushed the medic away several times to snarl at him and give him an evil glare.

"Just don't bite," Reilly warned me. "If you nip him and turn him into one of your lot, you'll be put down like a rabid dog, no excuses."

The medic wiped sweat from his forehead and I realized he was more nervous than I was. He was wearing thick gloves, but as I'd seen in the room when the woman bit the tall guy in leathers, clothes and gloves aren't foolproof against a zombie attack.

I tried to control myself after that, and didn't pull back as much as I had been doing, even though every part of me wanted to.

The medic left once he'd finished. I ran my tongue around my mouth and winced as one of my teeth nicked it.

"I should have warned you about that," Reilly said. "Doesn't matter how much you file them down, they'll always be sharper than they were. Best thing is to keep your tongue clear of your teeth."

"Thash eashy fuhr you tuh shay," I mumbled.

"Hey, not bad for your first attempt," Reilly said, looking impressed. "Most of the revitalizeds take a few days to get their act together. I think you're going to be a fast learner."

"Shkroo you, arsh hohl," I spat, and his expression darkened.

"Maybe you were better off mute," he growled.

It took me a while to get the hang of my new teeth. I still slur the occasional word, but a week into my new life–or unlife, or whatever the hell it's called–I can speak as clearly as I could before I was killed.

"B Smith went to mow, went to mow a meadow," I sing tunelessly to my reflection. "But a zombie ripped her heart out, so now she's a walking dead-o."

Hey, I might be dead, but you've gotta laugh, haven't you? Especially when you're no longer able to cry your bloody eyes out.

THREE

Lying on the bed, staring at the ceiling, thinking about Mum and Dad.

Reilly hasn't told me anything about the outside world. We've spent a lot of time together. He chats with me about all sorts of things, soccer, TV shows we used to watch, our lives before the zombie uprising. But he won't discuss the attack on my school or any of the other assaults that took place that day. I've no idea if order has been restored or if the soldiers and medics here are the only people left alive in the whole wide world. I've pushed him hard for answers, but although Reilly's been good to me, he can play deaf and dumb to perfection when he wants.

I've said a few prayers for Mum and Dad, even though I'm not the praying type. For Mum especially. It's strange. I thought I loved Dad more. He was the one I respected, the one I wanted to impress. Mum was weak in my opinion, a coward and a fool for letting her husband knock her about the place. I stood up for her and always tried to help when he'd lay into her, because that's what you do for your mum, but if you'd ask me to name a favorite, I'd have chosen Dad, despite all his flaws.

But she's the one I miss most. Maybe it's because of what Dad did the day I died. He came to rescue me. Risked his own life to try to save me. But then he made me throw Tyler to the zombies, turned me into a killer, and since then...

No. That's a lie, and I don't want to lie to myself anymore. I've done too much of that in the past. Be truthful, B. Dad didn't force me. I threw Tyler to the zombies because I was scared and it was the easy thing to do.

Dad hated foreigners and people who had different beliefs. I never wanted to be like him in that respect, but to keep him quiet I acted as if I was, and in the end it rubbed off on me. I became a monster. I don't ever want to allow that to happen again, but if I'm to keep the beast inside me under control, I have to accept that the guilt was mine for doing what Dad told me to do. You can't blame other people for sins of your own making.

I sit up, swing my legs off the bed and scowl. No use worrying about Mum and Dad until I have more information. I'm sure answers will be revealed in time. They can't be keeping me alive just to hold me in this cell forever. I have to be patient. Explanations will come. If I have to mourn, I'll do it once their deaths are confirmed. Until then I need to hope for the best.

To distract myself, I focus on the throbbing noise. It's constant, the rumbling of machines in the distance, AC, oxygen being pumped in for the living. It never ceases. It drove me mad for the first few days, but now I find it comforting. Without a TV, iPod, or anything else, it's the only way I have of amusing myself when Reilly's not around. I tune into the hum when I'm bored and try to put images to the noises, to imagine what's happening outside this cell, soldiers marching, medics conducting their experiments, the teenagers in leather....

Hmm. I've no idea who they were. I'm pretty sure, judging by the green moss on the tall guy's cheek, that they're like me, zombies who can think and act the way they did before they died. Reilly refers to us as *revitalizeds*. The ordinary, mindless zombies are *reviveds*. But why were the revitalizeds in that room with weapons? Are they prisoners like me, or are they cooperating with the soldiers? Where did they come from? Why are they—we—different from the others? Is there hope for us? Can we be cured?

I sneer at that last question. "Of course you can't be cured, you dumb bitch," I snort. "Not unless you can find the Wizard of Oz to give you a brand-new heart."

I get up and stand in front of the mirror. I seem to be studying myself a lot recently. It's not that I'm vain. There just isn't anything else to do. But I'm not interested in my face this time. I was wearing the shredded, filthy remains of my school uniform when I regained consciousness. That's been replaced with a pair of jeans and a plain white T-shirt.

I pull the T-shirt up to my chin and stare at my ruined chest. I never had big tits. Vinyl used to call them bee stings. I told him I'd do worse than sting him if he kept on saying that, but I liked Vinyl, so I let him get away with it.

My right boob is the same as it was before. But my left is missing, torn from my chest by Tyler Bayor. A fair bit of the flesh around it is missing too. And my heart's been ripped out, leaving an unnatural, grisly hole in its place.

Bits of bone poke through the flesh around the hole, and I can see all sorts of tubes inside, veins, arteries and what-have-you. Congealed blood meshes the mess together, along with the green moss that sprouts lightly all over the wound. Every so often a few drops of blood ooze out of one of the tubes. But it's not like it used to be. This blood is much thicker, the consistency of jelly, and the flow always stops after a second or two.

I quizzed Reilly about that. Without a heart, there shouldn't be any flow at all. The same way that, without working lungs, I shouldn't be able to speak.

"The body remembers," he said. "At least it does in revitalizeds."

"What the hell does that mean?" I frowned.

"When you recovered your wits, your brain started trying to

control the rest of your body, the way it did when you were alive," he explained. "You don't need to breathe anymore, but your brain thinks that you should, so it forces your lungs to expand and collapse, which is why you can talk. You can stop it when you focus – if you shut your mouth and close your nose, your lungs will shut down after a minute or two – but most of the time your lungs work away in the background, even though there's no reason why they should.

"If you had a heart, it would be the same. Your brain would tell it to pump blood around your body. It wouldn't operate as smoothly as it did before – no more than a weak pulse every few minutes – but it would keep the blood circulating, albeit sluggishly.

"Now, you don't have a heart," Reilly said unsympathetically, "but the brain's a stubborn organ and it's doing the best it can. It's roped in some of your other organs and is using them to nudge your veins and arteries, to compensate for the missing pump. Some of the scientists here are blown away by that. They've never seen a body do it before. They think you're the coolest thing since sliced bread. They'd love to take you off to their labs to study you in depth."

"Who's stopping them?" I asked, but at that the soldier clammed up again.

I've poked my finger into the cavity in my chest a few times, dipped it in the blood and smeared it across my tongue. But I can't tell if it tastes any different. My taste buds have gone to hell. My mouth is dry – my tongue feels like it's made of sandpaper – and apart from a foul staleness that is always there, I haven't been able to identify any specific tastes.

I sigh as I stare at the hole. It shocked me the first few times. I couldn't believe that was really me. I turned my back on the image and tried to cry. Shook my head and refused to accept that this was what I'd become. But now it doesn't bother me that much. I don't let it. Why should I? After all...

"Heh," I laugh humorlessly at my reflection.

...life's too short!

FOUR

Reilly comes in with a bowl. "Grub's up," he says cheerfully, kicking the door closed behind him. I'm standing in one of the corners when he enters, so I spot the armed soldiers outside the door as it slides shut. Reilly must have been coming to see me daily for at least two weeks, usually twice a day, but they never take chances. He always has backup in case I make a break for freedom. The soldiers outside couldn't save him if I decided to bite or give him a playful scratch, but they can make sure I don't get more than a couple of steps outside the cell.

"What's on the menu today?" I ask sarcastically.

"Lamb chops."

"Really?" I gasp.

"No, you idiot," he grunts, and hands the bowl to me.

I stare at lumps of cold gray meat in a jellyish substance. It's the same thing he's given me every day.

"I'm sick of this," I mutter.

"You will be in a minute," he laughs, then scratches his head. "What difference does it make? You can't taste anything anyway."

"It has no substance," I sniff. "I might not be able to taste it, but I can feel it as I grind it up, and it feels like frogspawn."

Reilly winks. "Maybe it is."

He's never told me what the meat is, just that it's laced with chemicals that will help me adjust.

"What would happen if I refused to eat it?" I ask.

Reilly shrugs. "You'd go hungry."

"So? It's not like I'm a growing girl, is it?"

"Trust me," Reilly says, "you don't want to go hungry. The dead feel hunger even worse than the living. Makes sense when you think about it. If you're alive and you starve, eventually you die and that's the end of your suffering. But if you're dead already, the pain goes on and on and on."

"Do you feed the reviveds too?" I ask.

"Just eat up, B. I don't have all day."

I know from experience that Reilly doesn't care whether I eat the gloop or not. I threw it back at him one day, to see how he'd react, if he'd try to force me to eat. He just shrugged, turned round, exited and let me go without.

I pick up the spoon at the side of the bowl and dip in. It took a while to get the hang of my new fingers. At first I tried picking up things with the bones sticking out of them. But I soon realized that I could grip like I did before, by using the remains of the flesh beneath the tips of my fingers. The bones aren't as much of an inconvenience as I thought they'd be. The only thing I can't do is close my hands into proper fists – the bones dig into my palms – but I can keep the fingers flat and bend them down until they touch my palms, and that's almost the same.

"What's happening in the world today?" I ask around spoonfuls of the cold, oily, slimy gruel. "Anything exciting?"

"Same as yesterday and the day before," Reilly answers glibly.

"What about the soccer? Do the zombies have a team in the Premier League?"

Reilly laughs. "I'd like to see that. *Undead United*!"

I grin and carry on eating. Reilly's all right as prison warders go. I don't trust him and I'm sure he'd fire a bullet through my head without a moment's hesitation if ordered. A day might come when we have to lock horns, and maybe one of us won't walk away from that clash. But he's treating me as humanely as he can – more than I probably would if our roles were reversed – and I appreciate that.

I spoon the last of the food into my mouth, chew a few times and swallow. "All done, boss."

"Like I give a damn," he says, taking the bowl from me. He crosses to the sink and picks up the bucket beneath it. Water was supplied to the taps once Reilly had warned me not to drink any of it, just use it for washing, and the bucket was put in place before he brought my first meal.

"Give me a minute," I grumble sourly. "I want to savor the moment."

I can no longer process food or drink the normal way. Reilly says it would sit in my guts, turn putrid and decay, unaided by any digestive juices. The bits that broke down into liquids would flow through me and dribble out, meaning I'd have to wear a diaper. The solids would stay inside me indefinitely. If I ate enough, they'd back up in my stomach and throat.

"Would that harm me?" I asked Reilly once.

"No," he said. "But maggots and worms would thrive on the refuse and insects would be attracted to it. You'd become a warren for creepy crawlies and they'd chew through you. They couldn't do any real damage unless they got into your brain and destroyed enough of it to kill you, but would you want to live like that?"

The image of insects burrowing through my flesh made me shiver so much that, if I hadn't been dead already, I would have sworn that somebody had walked over my grave.

I can safely eat the specially prepared food that Reilly gives me, but I can't keep the bulk of it down. According to Reilly, when the scientists first started to experiment, they used intravenous tubes to feed nutrients to the zombies. He said that's still the best way, but since most people prefer to eat, the good folk in the labs came up with a way for us to act as if we were still capable of enjoying a meal. The gray crud is designed to release nutrients into our clogged-up bloodstream almost instantly. But we have to get rid of the rest by ourselves.

"Come on," Reilly says, tapping a foot. "You're not the only one I have to deal with."

"I won't do it until you tell me how many others you look after."

"Doesn't bother me," Reilly says, turning away. "You're the one who has to live with the stink and insects."

"Wait," I stop him. Pulling a face, I lean over the bucket and stick a finger down my throat, careful not to tear the soft lining. The gray stuff comes surging back up and I vomit into the bucket, shuddering as I spit the last dregs from my lips.

"Not very ladylike, is it?" I grunt as I pass the bucket to a smiling Reilly.

"I don't think you were ever in danger of being mistaken for a lady," he says, "even when you were one of the living."

"I could sue you for saying that sort of thing to me," I huff.

"Lawyers don't represent corpses," he smirks.

I snarl at the grinning soldier and gnash my teeth warningly, but Reilly knows I'm not dumb enough to bite him. One of the first things he told me was that I can still be decommissioned, even though I'm already dead. As I already knew, zombies need their brains to function.

Even if they didn't want to kill me, they could punish me in other ways. I don't feel as much pain as I used to, but I'm not completely desensitized. I dug one of my finger bones into my flesh, to test myself, and it hurt. When I pushed even farther, it hurt like hell. The dead can be tortured too.

"By the way," Reilly says just before he exits. "You'll be entertaining a couple of visitors shortly, so be on your best behavior."

"Who's coming?" I snap, thinking for a second that it's Mum and Dad, torn between delight and terror at the thought. Part of me doesn't want them to see me like this. If they're alive, that part would rather they believed I was dead.

"You keep asking questions," Reilly says. "About the attacks, revitalizeds, why you're different to reviveds, how you wound up here. These people can give you some answers."

"Reilly!" I shout as he steps outside. "Don't leave me hanging like that. Tell me who..."

But the door has already closed. I'm locked in, alone and ignorant, as I have been for most of my incarceration.

But not for much longer if Reilly's to be believed.

FIVE

The visitors are a doctor and a soldier.

The doctor is a thin, balding man with a carefully maintained pencil mustache. He squints a lot, like someone who needs glasses but refuses to admit it. He didn't tell me his name when he entered, or even acknowledge my presence. He just stood with his hands crossed in front of him until a table and chair were put in place, then sat and said stiffly, "I am Dr. Cerveris."

The soldier is friendlier. He brought in the table, set it down, then went out to fetch the chairs. He also brought through a mobile TV and DVD player. At first I thought he was a regular soldier, but when he sat down with the doctor and nodded to let him know it was time to begin, I realized he must be someone important.

"I'm Josh Massoglia," he introduced himself, smiling widely. "But you can stick with Josh. Everybody else does. No one can pronounce my surname. I even struggle with it myself sometimes."

Josh laughed and I smiled. He's a good-looking guy, in a rugged kind of way. Hard to tell what color his hair is, since it's shaved down to the roots. He wears a plain green sweater over his shirt and acts like he's just one of the guys, but he has an air of authority. Dr. Cerveris is snooty, like someone who thinks he's a VIP. Josh is more laid-back, so comfortable with his power that he doesn't feel like he needs to prove anything.

The doctor pulls on a pair of thick plastic gloves and asks if he can examine me. I stand still while he prods and probes my fingers and face. I hesitate when he asks me to take off my T-shirt. Josh grins and turns away. I still feel awkward–I never liked undressing in front of doctors or nurses–but I disrobe as requested.

"Remarkable," Dr. Cerveris murmurs as he studies the wretched hole where my heart once beat.

"Take a photo if you like it that much," I grunt.

"I've already seen lots of snapshots of it," he says.

I frown, wondering when the photos were taken, but I don't ask.

Dr. Cerveris sits again and Josh turns his chair around.

"You've taken to this like a duck to water," Josh notes.

"You mean being dead?"

"Yeah. Most revitalizeds struggle. It takes a lot of counseling

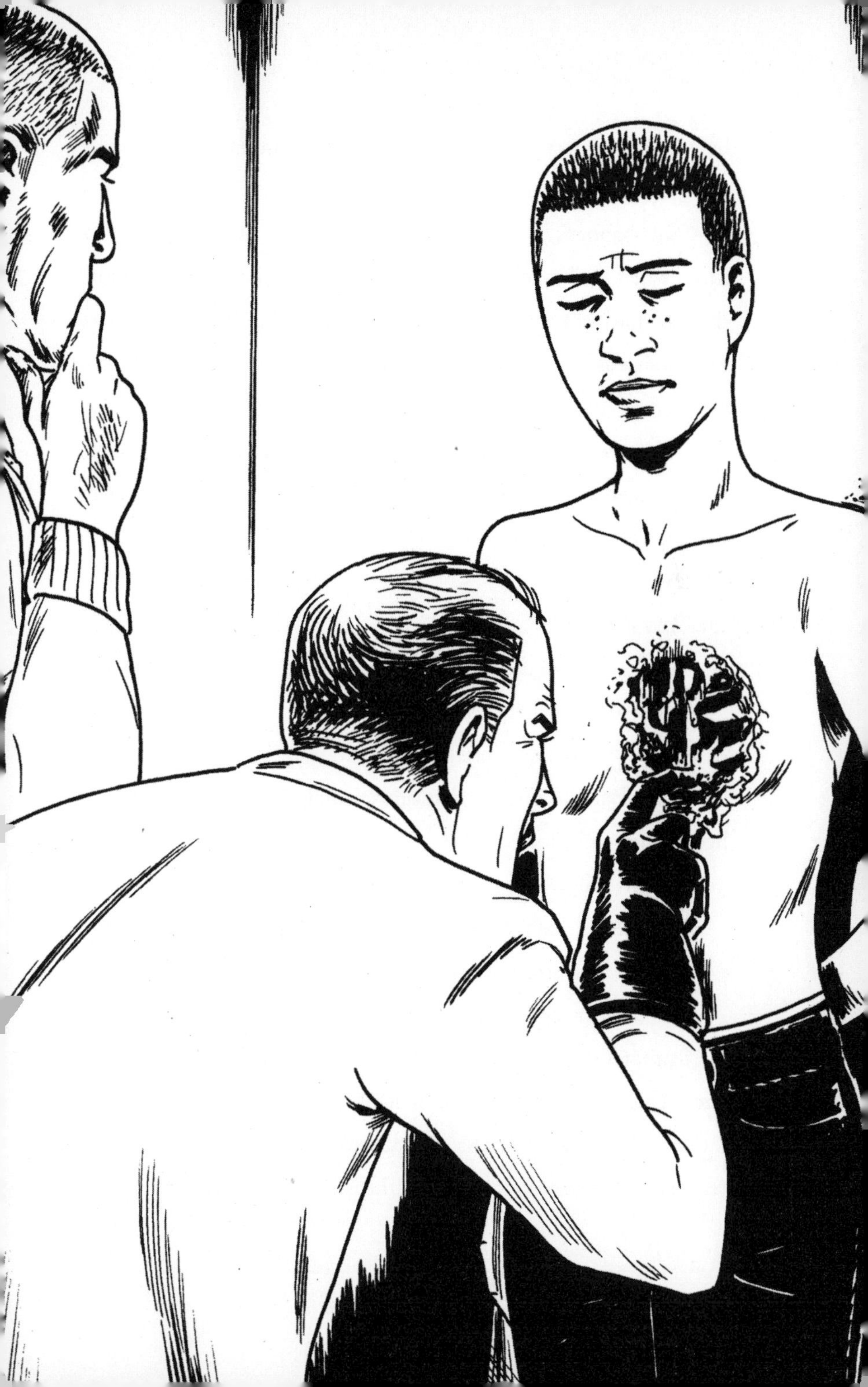

before they begin to adapt to their new circumstances. But you..." He whistles admiringly.

"Shit happens," I sniff, not telling him that of course there are times when I want to scream and sob, but that I don't plan to give these bastards the pleasure of seeing me crumble. "So are there a lot of revitalizeds?" I ask casually.

"A few," Josh replies vaguely.

"We haven't been able to establish an estimated ratio of revitalizeds to reviveds," Dr. Cerveris says. "But from what we have witnessed, only a fraction of the undead populace appears to recover consciousness."

"Any idea why?"

"We have some theories," he says.

"Care to share them with me?"

"No."

I scowl at the doctor, then glance at Josh. "How long have I been here?"

"In this cell?"

"No. *Here.*" I wave a hand around, indicating the entire complex. "How long since the attack on the school?"

"Six months, give or take," Josh says.

I process that glumly. Half a year of my life that I can never get back. This is one of those times when I feel very small and alone, but I don't let them see that. "Do all revitalizeds take that long to recover?" I ask instead, acting like the gap in my life is no big thing.

"No," Dr. Cerveris says. "Most revitalize sooner."

"My teachers always used to tell me that I was slow," I grin. "Have I been here all the time since I was killed?"

Josh nods. "We brought you here directly from the school. You were in a holding cell with other reviveds before your senses kicked back in."

"There were more attacks that day. My dad told me it was happening all over London."

Josh sighs. "Yeah. It wasn't a day any of us will forget in a hurry."

"Have there been more assaults since then?" I press. "Are zombies still striking or have you put a stop to it? What's the world like out there?"

Josh shakes his head. "I can't discuss that with you. All I can say is that the situation is currently stable."

"That doesn't tell me much," I huff.

"I know, but that's the way it is. There are limits to what we can discuss. If it's any comfort, we don't tell the other revitalizeds any more than we're telling you."

"Is there a reason why you're being so secretive?" I ask.

Josh rolls his eyes. "You're a flesh-eating member of the walking dead with the ability to convert as many of the living as you can get your hands or teeth on. You scare the living hell out of us. If some of our staff had their way, we'd tell you nothing at all, only incinerate every damn one of you."

"Why don't you?" I challenge him.

Dr. Cerveris answers. "We want to learn more about you, understand what makes you tick, why your memories return, if your current state is sustainable."

I stiffen. "You mean it might not be? I could...what's the word?"

"Regress." He nods somberly. "It has happened to a couple of others."

"That's why I came packing," Josh says, tapping a gun that hangs by his side. "You'd better pay attention and stay alert. If you start to zone out, the way you might in a boring class, I'm not going to take any chances. If I think there's even a slight chance that you're turning back into a revived, I'll put a bullet through your head."

"I bet you say that to all the girls," I snarl, and Josh laughs.

Dr. Cerveris asks lots of questions, about my past, how much of the day of the attack I can recall, if I can remember anything since then. Somebody opens the door and hands him a folder—he didn't call for it, so others must be watching this on hidden cameras—and he subjects me to a Rorschach test, then word-association games and other psychological crap. I play along patiently, answering honestly, in the hope that if I help them, they can find a way to help me.

The doctor asks about my sense of taste and smell. I tell him I can smell even better than before, but I can't taste anything.

"Is that strange?" I ask.

"No," he says. "The others are the same. We're not sure why.

What about your ears? Have you noticed any difference where sounds are concerned?"

"I dunno. There hasn't been much for me to listen to."

A machine is rolled in and Dr. Cerveris tests my hearing. He puts headphones on me and I have to raise my hand when I hear a high-pitched noise in either ear.

"How'd I do?" I ask when he takes them off.

"Admirably," he says. "Every revitalized has an improved sense of hearing. The reviveds do too. Your sense of smell is probably sharper as well, as you have noted. We'll test that some other time."

I grin ghoulishly. "So I've turned into a big bad wolf. All the better to see, hear and smell you with, my dear."

"Not *see*, I think," he mutters, and lo and behold, an eye chart is duly carried in by a soldier. The test tells me what I already knew, that my eyesight has deteriorated. It's not as bad as I feared. I can still make out most of the letters, even on the lower lines, but they're more blurred than they used to be.

"Would I go blind if I didn't put the drops in every day?" I ask.

"No," Dr. Cerveris says as he jots down the results. "We haven't observed any of the reviveds losing their sight completely. But they suffer irritation and infection. It gets so annoying in some that they scratch their eyes out."

I wince and immediately try to push the image from my thoughts. I'm glad I can't sleep because I'm sure I'd have nightmares about that if I did.

"A little knowledge can be a dangerous thing," Josh chuckles. "That's another reason we prefer not to tell you too much about yourself."

"I'd rather know than live in ignorance." I lean forward. Josh pats his gun and I stop and raise my palms. "Easy, boss. I wasn't trying to freak you out."

"Like I said before, I won't take any chances." The light tone is gone from his voice. "Any move towards us will be interpreted as an aggressive gesture, so just hold on the way you were and everything will be fine."

I ease back, hands still raised. "I just wanted to ask if you knew what caused the attacks, how this is happening, why the dead came back to life."

"That's classified," Josh says shortly.

"I figured as much, but if you don't ask..."

There's silence while Dr. Cerveris writes up his findings. A couple of soldiers enter and remove everything that had been brought through, except the TV and DVD player.

"What now?" I ask, trying to sound chirpy but failing.

Josh raises an eyebrow at Dr. Cerveris. The doctor stares at his notes, hands flat on the table. Then he looks at me. "I think it will be safe to introduce you to the other revitalizeds soon."

"The kids I saw dressed in leather?"

"Yes."

"The ones who were torturing the zombies?"

Dr. Cerveris smiles icily. I thought he'd deny the charge and say that wasn't what they were doing. But all he says is, "Yes."

"But don't refer to them as revitalizeds," Josh warns me. "They prefer to call themselves *zom heads*."

"Dig that crazy new slang," I mutter witheringly. "What happens after I've joined the merry gang? Where do I go from there?"

Josh frowns. "I don't understand what you're asking."

"What's an average day like for a zom head? Do we torment zombies all the time? Go on picnics? Hang around looking cool in our leathers?" I start to lean forward, recall Josh's warning and stop myself. "What does the future hold? Do I have any chance of being set free?"

Dr. Cerveris and Josh share a smug look. It's as if they've been waiting for me to ask that question. Without a word, Dr. Cerveris turns to the TV and switches it on.

As the TV flickers to life, Josh turns on the DVD player and presses play. A grainy black-and-white image comes into focus. It's a corridor in my old school. Kids in uniform run past what must have been a security camera. Others follow, but although these look the same as the first lot, I can tell that they're zombies by the way they move. They don't shuffle along like zombies in movies, but move intently, swiftly, surely, like hunters.

Josh rewinds. He lets it play again, then pauses as the pack of zombies comes into view. "Spot anyone you know?"

"I didn't realize we were playing *Where's Waldo?*" I snap.

"Actually it's *Where's Becky Smith?*" he corrects me, and points to the lower left of the screen.

I stare hard, but with my weakened eyesight I can't be sure. It looks like me, but the picture quality isn't great and I'm not used to seeing myself in black-and-white.

"This next clip is from a helmet camera," Josh informs me. "I wasn't one of those who stormed your school, but I was part of the control team coordinating various units across London. One of my guys captured this charming footage."

He hits play again and the black-and-white clip gives way to a shaky color shot. The person with the camera is moving swiftly, jerking his head from side to side. I glimpse a rifle in his hands.

Horror images. Blood sprayed across walls. Limbs and corpses scattered across the floor. There's a blur. The rifle kicks in the soldier's hand. The camera goes out of focus for a few seconds. When it steadies again, I find myself looking at a kid whose head has been blown apart. Hard to tell if it was a boy or a girl. It's just scraps of meat now.

The soldier pushes on, then pauses. He focuses on a number of bodies to his left. I thought they were all corpses, but someone's moving in among the dead. The soldier takes a few steps forward, stops and adjusts the camera. It zooms in on the face of a zombie hunched over the remains of a dead boy.

The zombie has cut the boy's head open and is digging out bits of his brain, spooning them into its mouth with its bone-distorted fingers. It looks like a drug addict on a happy high. The boy's arms are still shaking—he must be alive, at least technically. The zombie doesn't care. It goes on munching, ignorant of the trembling arms, the soldiers, everything except the slivers of brain.

The zombie is a girl.

The zombie is *me*.

"We don't know how many you killed that day," Josh says softly, "but by the variety of flesh and blood we picked out of your mouth when we were hosing you down later, we're pretty sure that boy wasn't the first."

"We can never release you, Becky," Dr. Cerveris says with just a hint of gloomy satisfaction. "You're a monster."

I don't respond. I can't. All I can do is keep my eyes pinned on the girl–the *monster*–on the screen. And stare.

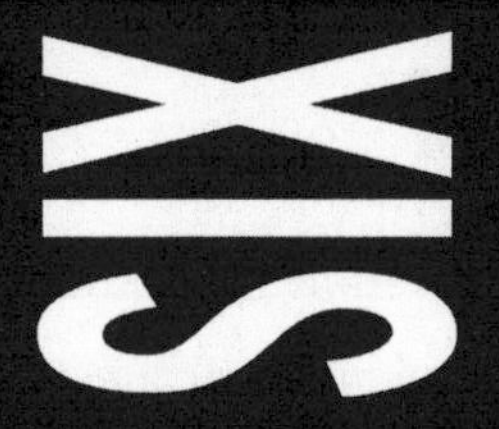

SIX

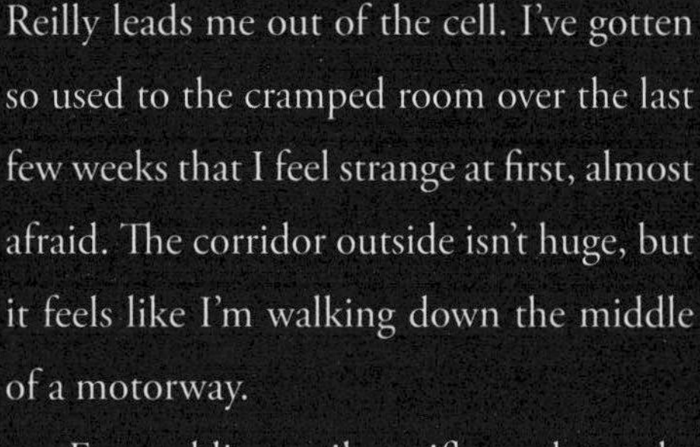

Reilly leads me out of the cell. I've gotten so used to the cramped room over the last few weeks that I feel strange at first, almost afraid. The corridor outside isn't huge, but it feels like I'm walking down the middle of a motorway.

Four soldiers trail us, rifles at the ready. They're mean-looking sons of bitches. I think they'd love an excuse to let rip. I keep my hands tight by my sides, head down, mincing along like a lamb.

Reilly wanted to let me out several days ago, not long after my meeting with Dr. Cerveris and Josh. He was stunned when I asked if I could stay in the cell a while longer. After what I'd seen on the TV, I needed some time by myself. I felt dirty and twisted, not fit to mix with anybody else, even zombies.

I spent the last few days lying on my bed or squatting in a corner, fixating on what I'd seen, the way I'd feasted. It shouldn't have come as a shock—I know what I am and what zombies do—but it did. I'd imagined what I thought was the worst, lots of times, but nothing could have prepared me for the cold, hard reality of that film footage.

I could have tried to wipe the memory from my thoughts, turned my back on it and pretended I'd never seen the macabre film. But I remember something my teacher Mr. Burke once said. "There are lots of black-hearted, mean-spirited bastards in the world. It's important that we hold them to account. But always remember that *you* might be the most black-hearted and mean-spirited of the lot, so hold yourself the most accountable of all."

After throwing Tyler to the zombies, I vowed that I'd change, that I'd spend the rest of my life trying to make up for what I'd done. But I can't do that if I don't accept the truth about myself. I'm a vicious, cannibalistic killer. I've done plenty to be ashamed of, and I owe it to my victims to face that shame and live with it, to never forget them or what I did.

After a lot of thinking, I came to terms with my guilt and... No, that's not right. I wasn't comfortable with what I'd done, and I hope I never will be. But I found a place within myself to house the horror, somewhere close to the surface but not so close that it would get in the way of everything else. Once I'd done that, I figured I was ready to face the world again. So when Reilly offered a second time to take me to see the revitalizeds, I agreed to tag along.

We wind through a series of corridors. They all look the same, white or gray walls, fluorescent lights, lots of windows and sealed doors. I peer through some of the windows and catch glimpses of soldiers, doctors, nurses, but nothing revealing.

By the control panels set in the walls next to the doors, I can tell that they're operated by scanners, one at waist height for fingerprints, the other higher up for retinas. Some of them require a security code too.

Reilly finally stops at a door, opens it with a quick scan of his fingers and an eye, then gestures for me to enter. I step in, expecting a load of leather-clad, teenage zombies, but it's only a shower room, several vacant cubicles, towels and clothes laid on a bench across from them.

"What gives?" I ask suspiciously.

"You've been in isolation for three weeks," Reilly says. "You haven't changed your clothes. I thought you might want to freshen up before you meet the others."

"Are you saying I smell?"

"Yes."

"No peeking," I warn him.

He laughs. "Zombies don't do it for me. But others will be watching." He nods at the ceiling. "Cameras all over this place, as I'm sure you've figured out already."

"Yeah. But I thought they'd leave the bloody showers alone."

Reilly shrugs and closes the door. I gaze around, trying to spot the cameras, but they're masterfully concealed. "Sod it," I mutter and undress. If some creep gets a buzz from watching a one-boobed zombie in the buff, more power to him.

The shower's lovely, though I have to turn it up to the max to truly appreciate it. My nerve endings don't work as well as they used to. I have to crank the heat up close to boiling before I feel warm.

I scrub carefully around the hole in my chest. I pick at the green moss and try to wash it away, but it must be rooted deeply. If I pull hard, strands come out like hairs, but I'm worried I might injure myself–I don't know how deeply the moss is embedded and I'm afraid I might rip an even bigger hole in my chest if I persist–so I stop. I rinse down the rest of my body, smiling sadly as I rub the old *c* scar on my thigh. I used to hate that, since it was my only real physical blemish. Now, with a missing heart, it's the least of my worries.

I massage shampoo into my scalp and try to close my eyes, forgetting that I can't. Scowling, I tilt my head back and do my best to keep the suds away from my unprotected eyeballs.

Stepping out, I towel myself dry. The moss stays damp, except for the light layer on my right wrist where I was scratched shortly before Tyler clawed out my heart—that dries up nicely after a good bit of rubbing.

Giving up on the moss around my chest, I slip into the new clothes. Once I'm cozy, I sniff the old set and grimace. They're not as bad as I thought they'd be, but I'm surprised I didn't notice the odor before. Reilly should have told me.

I rap on the door and it opens immediately. "Any deodorant?" I ask.

Reilly cocks his head. "Are you being funny?"

"No."

"Didn't they tell you...?" He smiles. "No, I suppose it's not the sort of thing they would have thought of. Well, it's good news, B. You don't ever have to worry about your pits again. The dead don't sweat."

"Seriously?"

"Yeah."

"Cool," I chuckle. Then a thought hits me and I ask with fake innocence, "What about bad breath?"

"There's a slight smell that will always be there," Reilly says. "But it won't get any worse than that."

"And farts?" I ask.

Reilly laughs. "No. You're clear on that front too."

"A pity," I sigh. "I loved a good fart." My eyes narrow and I murmur sweetly, "What about my period?"

Reilly blushes furiously. "Without a regular flow of blood? Hardly!"

"But are you sure?" I press.

"Well, not a hundred percent," he says uneasily.

"Can you ask one of the nurses and find out for me?" I tease him.

"Ask them yourself," he huffs, ears reddening at the thought of it.

Typical bloke—so easy to embarrass!

SEVEN

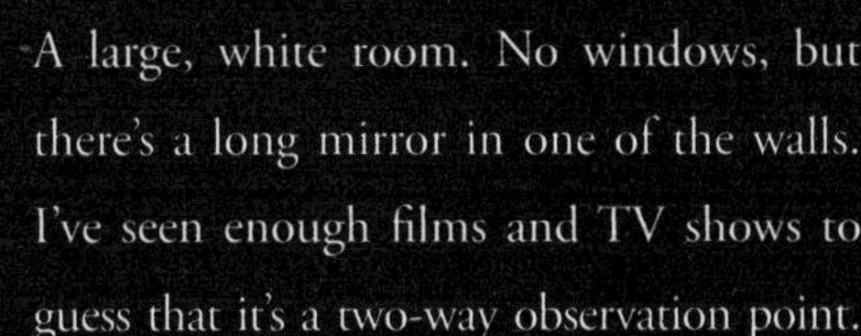

A large, white room. No windows, but there's a long mirror in one of the walls. I've seen enough films and TV shows to guess that it's a two-way observation point. I bet there's a team of soldiers or scientists on the other side, watching everything.

There's a pool table and a ping-pong table down at one end of the room. A bookshelf with a scattering of books, magazines and comics. A couple of TVs, one hooked up to a DVD player, the other to a video-game console. There's a table close to that TV, loaded with games and a few iPods. A variety of couches and chairs are positioned around the place.

A couple of the zom heads are playing pool. Three are busy gaming. One – the girl called Cathy – is watching TV and

filing down her teeth. And the final zom head is slumped on a chair near the bookshelf, flicking through a car magazine.

Seven in total. One more than I saw in the room all those weeks ago.

I hover by the door–Reilly didn't say anything when he let me in–waiting for the others to notice me. Finally one of the guys playing pool looks up and shouts, "Hey! It's the girl who kicked Rage's arse!"

Everything comes to a stop and those who were sitting stand up to ogle me, all except the one in the chair with the magazine. He just glances at me, yawns, then returns to his mag.

I push forward, smiling awkwardly. "Hi. I'm Becky Smith, but everyone calls me B."

"Becky it is," one of the boys laughs, and jogs across. He sticks out a hand—it's covered by a glove and bandages. "I'm Mark," he says as we shake hands. "I wasn't there when you revitalized. They keep me out of stuff like that. Afraid I'll react badly to the flames."

"What do you mean?" I ask.

The boy gestures at himself. He's covered completely from neck to toe, heavy clothes, some sort of a padded vest, more bandages, heavy-duty boots. "I got burned to the bone while I was a revived. They don't know how. My face is okay but I'm like a skeleton under all these layers. I have to stay wrapped up. They're worried that if I lose any more internal–"

"Can it, Worm," one of the other boys says. "You'd bore her to death if she wasn't already dead." He nods at me but doesn't smile. He's dark-skinned, with short curly hair. I would have shot him the finger six months ago in response to his nod. But since I'm trying to change and accept everyone as an equal, no matter what color they are, I nod back at him instead.

"B," I tell him.

"I know," he says drily. "I'm not deaf. I'm Peder."

"Danny," the boy beside him says. Danny's tall and bony. Greasy blond hair and bad acne. He's wearing jeans and a T-shirt like mine. As I look around, I see that all of the others are similarly dressed, except for the guy in the chair. He's in the leathers he was wearing when I first saw him.

"Cathy Kelly," the girl introduces herself coldly. She sits and focuses on the video game. She has long, dark hair tied back in a ponytail. Pretty, but not in a soft way.

One of the other boys comes over and shakes my hand. "Gokhan."

"*Gherkin*?" I frown.

"Gokhan." He spells it out. "Turkish, innit?"

He's plump and relaxed-looking. Olive skin. Large, pudgy fingers. He's filed down the bones sticking out of the tips and painted them with swirling, colorful designs.

"And I'm Tiberius," the other guy who was playing pool says. He's the one who first spotted me. He's short, with ginger hair and loads of freckles.

"Tiberius?" I laugh automatically. "What sort of a dumb name is that?"

"I was named after the river Tiber in Rome," he says stiffly. Then he turns his back on me, offended, and snaps at Mark, "Are you playing or what, Worm?"

"In a minute," Mark says. "I want to show B round first. Don't you want to get to know her? She's one of us now."

"Maybe she is and maybe she isn't," the boy in the chair says. He finally stands, cracks his knuckles over his head and makes a yawning motion. I know from practicing in my cell that we can mimic the habits of the past, when we had a set of fully functioning lungs. I even find myself yawning or sneezing by accident sometimes, my body remembering happier, simpler days.

The yawning knuckle cracker is the tall guy with the big head and small ears, the chubby, rosy cheeks, a chunk bitten out of the left one. The guy I clobbered over the head when I first recovered. *Rage.*

"Of course she's one of us," Mark says. "She can talk, can't she?"

"Oh, she's a revitalized," Rage says, eyeing me beadily. "Doesn't mean she's a zom head though. You've gotta earn that right. Which *you* haven't yet, Worm, in case you'd forgotten."

Mark scowls and stares at his feet. "It's not my fault they don't let me join in with the rest of you. I would if I could. You know that."

"You say that you would," Rage sneers. "But there's saying and there's doing, and so far you've done zip. For all we know, you've cried off and asked to be excused regular duties. Maybe the burns are a sham. Maybe they're just saying that because you asked them to cover up for the fact that you're a coward."

Mark stiffens, then squares himself and raises his fists. His hands are shaking, more with fear, I think, than indignation. "Say that again and I'll thump you," he squeaks. "I don't care how big you are."

Rage laughs. "Back down, Worm. I'm only messing with you."

He comes closer and circles me slowly. I say nothing while I'm being examined. When he's finished, I stare at him calmly. "Like what you see?"

"Not a lot," he sniffs. "I don't think Cathy has much to worry about."

"Why should I be worried?" the girl barks, looking up from her game.

"You've been queen bee round these parts," Rage says. "You know that all the boys fancy you, since they've no one else to lust after. Nobody would want to lose that sort of a following. And I don't think you will. No offense, *Becky*."

"Get stuffed," I snarl.

Rage cocks his head. "Are you a tough girl?" he whispers. "You are, aren't you? A fighter, yeah?"

"Wind me up and find out," I challenge him, fingers curling by my sides.

Rage glances at my fingers, then studies my eyes. "Looks like I was wrong. You *are* one of us."

"We accept you, gooble gobble," Tiberius chuckles from beside the pool table.

"What the hell does that mean?" I growl.

"Pay no attention to him," Gokhan laughs. "He's always coming out with weird crap like that."

"It's from *Freaks*," Tiberius says. "That old movie about circus freaks." He looks around for support. "Some of you must have seen it."

"Was it black-and-white?" Cathy asks.

"Yeah. It was made in the 1930s."

"Then of course we haven't seen it," she snorts. "We don't all waste our time on boring old movies."

"*Freaks*, boring?" Tiberius roars. "It's an amazing film. They used real-life freaks. It gave me nightmares the first time my dad showed it to me."

"They'd probably have found a role for *you* in it if you'd been alive back then," Cathy says frostily.

Tiberius glares at her, then turns to me. "Anyway, at one point a normal woman marries one of the freaks and they have a big party to welcome her into the family. They all start chanting, *We accept you, gooble-gobble.* They mean it nicely, but what they're really saying is that she's one of them now, a freak, an outcast, a child of the damned."

Tiberius bends over the pool table to take a shot, then says again, but glumly this time, as if he feels sorry for me, "We accept you, gooble-gobble."

EIGHT

I spend the rest of the day with the zom heads, getting to know them. It's awkward. None of us wants to be here. We haven't chosen each other for company. We come from different parts of London, Danny from as far out as Bromley. We don't have much in common, except for the fact that we were all killed when the zombies attacked.

"Do you remember much about that day?" I ask Mark. I'm with him, Gokhan and Tiberius on one of the couches close to the mirror.

"No," he says. "I was at school. Things went mad. I was running. I didn't even know why. I was part of a pack, doing what everybody else was. I thought someone had a gun and was shooting people, like they do in America. Then something struck the side of my head and I blacked out. Next thing I knew, I was waking up here, wrapped up tighter than a bloody Mummy."

"What about you?" I ask the others.

They shake their heads.

"We've gone over this dozens of times," Tiberius says. "It was pretty much all we talked about for the first few weeks. Everyone was at school, except Rage, who was in a shopping center with his girlfriend. Zombies attacked. We were bitten. We revitalized here."

"Were you locked into your school?"

Tiberius frowns. "What?"

"The exits were blocked in mine. We couldn't get out."

"What, someone actually stopped you from escaping?" Mark gasps.

"Yeah. We tried two different doors and they were both jammed. What about the mutants?"

"Come again?" Tiberius asks.

"There were mutants at our school, coordinating the zombies, directing them."

"Bull," he snorts.

"No, I'd seen a couple of them before. Ugly mothers with gray hair and yellow eyes. They all wear hoodies."

"You're dreaming," Tiberius insists.

"I'm dead," I snap. "We don't dream."

Tiberius clicks his tongue against his teeth. "So, what, you're saying the attacks were deliberate? That we were targeted?"

"I dunno," I shrug. "I'm just telling you what I saw."

"Hey, Rage, have you heard about this?" Tiberius yells and makes me repeat my story.

"Anybody else see hooded mutants?" Rage asks the rest of the zom heads once I'm done. Everyone's staring at me, having stopped whatever they were doing to listen.

"I didn't see any mutants," Peder says, "but one of the exit doors at my school was locked. I was furious. I'd gone through hell to make it that far. I kept kicking and punching it until the zombies swarmed me." He rubs his upper right arm, where a deep cut runs from the shoulder down to his elbow.

"It's something we wondered about before," Danny says. "How did the zombies get inside the buildings in the first place? Why were there so many of them? Where did they come from? Some of us think we might have been victims of a conspiracy."

"Terrorists," Cathy whispers.

"Get real," I laugh. "You can't think this was a terrorist attack. What, they got sick of bombs and guns, decided to use zombies instead?"

"Chemical warfare," Cathy says seriously. "It's something that terrorists have been exploring for years. Maybe they found a way to reanimate the dead. I mean, unless it's some sort of freak disease, *somebody* must have set those undead bastards loose on us."

"It could have been aliens," Mark suggests.

Tiberius nods enthusiastically. "That's my vote."

"That's why you're a pair of airheads," Rage jeers. "Aliens! Cathy's right. It was probably cooked up by mad scientists. Whether they were working for foreign powers or not, I don't know. I think it might have been our own guys, that it got leaked accidentally."

"If that was the case, they wouldn't have just struck at the schools," Cathy argues.

"They didn't," Rage responds. "I was in a shopping mall. I heard that there had been attacks at hospitals, airports, all sorts of places."

"Yeah, *attacks*," Cathy presses. "If it was an accidental breakout, it would have spread from one spot and rippled outwards. But they struck all over London at the same time. Explain that, if it wasn't planned."

There's a troubled silence. I'm disappointed that nobody seems to know any more than I do. I was hoping to find answers, but the zom heads are victims like me, ignorant of what really happened.

"Anybody know if the zombies are still running wild out there?" I ask.

"They don't tell us stuff like that," Peder says. "They don't even tell the teacher's pet what's going on outside, do they, Rage?"

"Bite me," Rage barks, and the others laugh.

"Why's he their pet?" I ask.

"He sucks up to them," Tiberius smirks.

"It's all, *Yes, Mr. Reilly, sir!* and, *No, Mr. Reilly, sir!*" Danny jeers.

"*Can I help you with anything, Dr. Cerveris?*" Gokhan adds. "*Do you want me to bend over, so you can stick your needle up my—*"

"One more word, eunuch boy, and it'll be your last for a while," Rage says softly, and the teasing stops instantly. He glares around and everyone drops their gaze. Except me.

"Something you want to say?" he growls.

"Yeah," I answer calmly. "Why'd you call him eunuch boy?"

Rage relaxes. "He's Turkish. Half of that lot are eunuchs."

"Hey!" Gokhan objects. "That's racist, innit?"

"Not if it's true," I smirk, and the others laugh. I grin for a moment. Then I recall Tyler and my vow to put my crude ways behind me, and my face drops. Looks like I'll have to try harder in the future. Old habits die hard.

"So nobody knows anything," I mutter. "We don't know how zombies came to be, why they attacked when they did, how they struck in so many different places at once, or what the upshot of it was. The undead might have all been killed or captured, or maybe they're still on the loose and this is the last place on earth where the living can walk around safely."

"It's not," Danny says confidently. "I overheard Reilly talking with one of the other soldiers. He was telling him to shape up or they'd ship him out to a different unit, one that wasn't as tightly secured as this place."

"Well done," Cathy says scathingly.

"What?" Danny whines.

She nods at the mirror. "You know that they're listening. You've just gone and dropped Reilly in it."

"Well, he's one of them," Danny sniffs. "I don't care what happens to him, just like he doesn't really care about any of us."

"Reilly's all right," Peder says.

"Yeah," Danny agrees, "but at the end of the day he's just doing his job. He treats us decently because he's told to. If they told him to put us down, you think he wouldn't?"

There's another long, uneasy silence.

"I thought you guys were better off than me," I say softly. "But you're not, are you? You're prisoners, just like I am."

"Yeah," Mark says when nobody else replies. "But it's not all bad. We could be reviveds. They keep them in huge holding cells, packed in tight together, none of the comforts that they treat us to. And they experiment on them. We don't have to deal with any of that."

"No?" Cathy laughs cruelly. "You're even dumber than I thought, Worm." She points at the mirror again. "What do you think all this is? We're guinea pigs, just like the reviveds. And when Dr. Cerveris and his crew have learned all that they can, we'll be discarded as casually as the others are."

We all stare at the mirror and wonder who's on the other side and what they might be thinking. Then we drift apart and everyone goes to their own part of the room to brood. Some of them shoot me dirty looks every so often, blaming me for reminding them that at the end of the day we're just fancily treated prisoners, at the mercy of those who have absolutely no human reason to show us any.

NINE

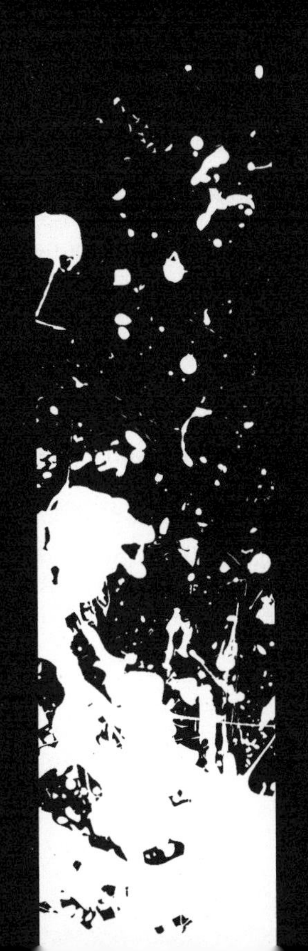

Reilly takes us back to our cells one at a time and leaves us there for what must be night. That develops into a routine. He escorts us to zom HQ (as we call it) every day, lets us mix for several hours, then returns us to our cells. We always go with him individually. Nobody ever gets to see where the other zom heads are housed. We could all be quartered in the same corridor, or in completely different parts of the complex—we've no idea.

They could leave us with each other the whole time–like me, the others don't need to sleep–but Tiberius thinks they're trying to institutionalize us, to make us easier to control.

I try to discuss the attacks and the outside situation again, but nobody wants to talk about that. They've been through it all before and are reluctant to rehash old arguments. It doesn't matter that all of the theories are fresh to me. They've been together for months now, and even though they're not tight like real friends, they share a bond that I'm not yet a true part of. They're not going to break their rules just to please the new zom head on the block.

Even Mark, the friendliest of the lot, gets prickly when I push him.

"Just leave it, B," he mutters. "What's the point? We can't do anything about it. If they want to tell us, they will. If they don't, they won't, and all the guessing in the world won't get us any closer to the truth."

Mark's the runt of the litter. The others tease him and pick on him, even Cathy. They call him Worm and mock him for not being allowed to join the zom heads when they experiment on reviveds. Mark takes it as best he can, laughs along with them, only occasionally grimaces when they go too far.

Danny tested me on my second day in zom HQ. Tossed a casual insult my way to see how I'd react.

"Say that again and you'll be picking the remains of your teeth out of your mouth," I told him, ready to back up the words with action if pushed. But Danny's no fool. He saw that I was serious and judged me a genuine threat, even though I'm a girl and he's bigger than me. Nobody's given me grief since then.

Rage is the undisputed leader of the pack. He's a big old bruiser—easy to see how he got his nickname—but clever too, reads a lot, excels at the more difficult video games, knows about all sorts of things. Reminds me a bit of my dad, a bully but sharp. It's hard to get the better of people like that. You can't beat them up and you can't outsmart them. Rage doesn't seem to be as violent as my dad, but he's not somebody you provoke lightly because there's always the chance that he'll snap and smash you up.

Having said that, he acts like a toad whenever any of the scientists or soldiers come to see us. I thought the others were exaggerating when they were winding him up that first day, but I soon see that they're not. He's like a fanboy when Josh or his team is on the scene.

Dr. Cerveris came this morning to run some routine tests on us, eyes, ears, that sort of thing. We get tested regularly, usually by nurses or low-level doctors. But today we were treated to a visit by the high and mighty one himself.

"Hey, Dr. Cerveris, how you been?" Rage beamed, running over to him like an eager puppy.

"Very well, thank you," the doctor replied, then asked Rage how things were going. Once they'd dispensed with the small talk, Rage barked at the rest of us and ordered us to line up. He walked down the line with Dr. Cerveris, glaring at us, making sure nobody said anything untoward or threatened the doctor in any way.

"Are those okay?" Rage asked when Dr. Cerveris came to the Turk and paused to study his painted finger bones.

"Yes," the doctor said. "I was just curious to see what he had drawn." He smiled at Gokhan. "You have an artistic eye."

"Art's my favorite subject, innit?" Gokhan replied.

"We'll have to give you oils and canvas, to see if your skills have been affected by your altered circumstances."

"I dunno about that," Gokhan pouted. "I'm not really into proper painting."

"You'll do whatever the hell the doctor tells you to do!" Rage roared, and shoved Gokhan in the chest.

Gokhan squared up to Rage and it looked like things were going to kick off, but Dr. Cerveris coughed politely and said, "Please, boys, no fighting."

I think Gokhan would have ignored him, but as soon as the doctor called for peace, Rage took a step back and muttered an apology.

"Why do you suck up to them so much?" I asked once Dr. Cerveris had left. I thought Rage would prickle at that but he only shrugged.

"They're the new masters now. If we're to have any hope of getting out of this place, we need to play ball. Besides, they've taken good care of us. We should be thankful. They could have left us to rot with the zombies. They're doing their best to look after us and make our lives easier. You don't bite the hand that feeds you."

I haven't seen much of the complex yet. Reilly never varies the route when he leads me to or from my cell. The others haven't seen much more of it either, though they've been to the places where the reviveds are housed.

According to Mark, there are hundreds, if not thousands, of zombies locked up in the pens. He thinks they're being held for experimental purposes. This is a giant laboratory, not a prison.

The reviveds are a mix of adults and children. But nobody's seen any grown-up zom heads. We've been segregated by age for some reason. There must be adult revitalizeds, conscious as we are, but they're either being held in a separate part of the complex or in a different building. I don't know why they'd want to divide us this way. Maybe they're worried that we'd start a big zom head family if they let us mix together freely.

There's no doubt that I'm an outsider–nothing personal, I'm sure it's purely because I'm new to the fold–but I was getting along all right with most of the zom heads until a couple of days ago. Cathy was the only one who actively disliked me. She wouldn't talk to me unless it was to say something critical. Then we had *hairgate* and I've been snubbed by the rest of them ever since.

I'd just finished filing down my teeth and was studying myself in the mirror. I ran a hand over the stubble on my head and muttered, "I hope this grows back soon. I fancy a change of style."

Cathy laughed hysterically. "Did you hear what dopey B said?" she cawed to the others.

"What's so funny about that?" I growled.

"You think your hair will grow back."

"Why the hell wouldn't...?" I stopped and groaned as I caught on.

"You're dead, dumbo," Cathy sneered. "Your hair won't ever grow again. You're stuck with that G.I. Jane look for life."

She kept on mocking me until I lost my cool. With a bellow, I rushed her, grabbed her ponytail and dragged her down onto the floor. She squealed and slapped at my hands but I was too strong for her. The others crowded round, egging us on.

"They don't let us have knives in here," I said, "but these bones sticking out of my fingers are every bit as good. If they can cut through skulls, hair shouldn't be much of a problem. I'm going to shave you even balder than I am, bitch."

"No!" Cathy screamed as I started hacking at her hair. "Don't, B, please!"

I ignored her and severed her ponytail. As it came free, I held it up in the air and whooped.

"Now for the rest of it," I jeered, waving my hand in front of her eyes, letting her see what I'd already cut away.

The fight drained from her when she saw her hair, and she started making loud moaning noises, the closest she could get to crying. I paused uneasily and watched her shaking. She reached out, took the hair from my fingers, clutched it to her chest and wailed, a dry, choking, wretched sound.

"Nice going," Tiberius snarled. "That won't grow back. She can never replace it."

"You didn't do much to stop me," I challenged him, and glared defiantly at the others, who were all looking a tad too self-righteous for my liking. "You just stood there, cheering."

"Yeah," Danny snorted. "That's right. Blame us. *You* cut off her hair, but *we're* the guilty ones."

"It's not that bad," I muttered. "I didn't scalp her."

They only stared at me with contempt until I turned my back on them and stomped away. Then they all crouched around Cathy and sympathized with her, conveniently forgetting the fact that she was the one who started the fight.

So much for my *friends*. Hypocritical jerks! I think I prefer being in my cell on my own.

TEN

In zom HQ. The others are still giving me the cold shoulder because of what I did to Cathy. I've tried apologizing but the snooty cow just ignores me. Sod her, the rest of them too. I don't care. Real loneliness is when your dad beats up your mum and you're lying in your bedroom, listening to her weep in the room next door, and it feels like the whole world's against you. A bunch of petty zombies giving me the evils? Doesn't bother me in the least.

The door opens and Reilly enters, Josh Massoglia just behind him. "You guys ready for some fun and games?" Josh roars.

"Damn right!" Rage bellows, rallying the others and shooing them towards the door. I haven't seen them this excited before.

"What about me?" Mark cries. "Can I come?"

"Sorry," Josh says. "We gave you the once-over a few days ago when we had you in for a checkup. The burns are still really bad. It's best you sit out this one."

"Don't worry, Worm," Rage chuckles. "We'll tell you all about it when we come home."

Mark looks crestfallen. If he could cry, he'd be blinking back tears.

As the others gather by the door, Josh looks over at me. "You just gonna sit there or do you want in on this too?"

"I'm invited?" I ask suspiciously, thinking it might be a trap.

"Of course," Josh says. "Why wouldn't you be?" He raises an eyebrow at Rage. "That's not a problem, is it?"

Rage smiles quickly. "Not at all. The more the merrier. Come on, B, hurry up, you don't want to make us late."

I'd like to tell the big lump to get stuffed, but I don't want to miss out on this. So I say nothing, only line up with the rest of them and follow Josh and Reilly out of zom HQ and into the heart of the complex.

Cathy cuddles up close to Josh as we're walking—well, as close as he'll let her, worried as he must be that she might accidentally scratch him and condemn him to living death. She makes cow eyes at him and actually asks if he's been working out. Give me strength! Josh laughs it off and pretends he doesn't know that she's got a crush on him.

We come to a door that requires a security code as well as the usual finger and retinal scans. Reilly opens it and we step into a room packed with weapons of all description. They're locked away in padlocked, thick steel cages, and I don't see any keys on either of the soldiers. Doesn't look like they want to take the chance of us going wild and getting our hands on a full arsenal.

Some of the weapons have been laid on a table in the middle of the room. "Take your pick," Josh says grandly. "Girls first."

I approach with Cathy and cast an eye over the loot. Flame-throwers, stun guns, spears, large knives, axes and small chainsaws. Two of each.

"Wow!" Cathy exclaims, rushing to grab a chainsaw. "These are new. They're awesome."

"Have you used a chainsaw before?" Josh asks.

"No."

"You'd better be careful. They're nasty if you swing them the wrong way. Maybe you should leave that to the boys."

"I'll be fine," Cathy smirks, pulling a cord to turn it on. She scythes through the air with the buzzing saw a couple of times, then turns it off and hangs it by her side. I hate to admit it, but she looks cool as hell.

"Becky?" Josh asks.

"I don't know." I study the weapons glumly. I've never used anything like this before. I'm worried that I'll pick something I can't use and end up looking like a mug. Maybe I should have stayed in zom HQ with Mark.

"We normally insist on pairs," Reilly explains. "Now that Cathy's chosen a chainsaw, somebody else has to choose one too. Usually, if you picked a flamethrower and Rage stepped up next and chose a knife, the final three would have to make their choice from those weapons, one each."

"But now there's seven of you," Josh says. "So there will have to be an odd one out. Tell you what, since this is your first time, you can have dibs on the exclusive weapon. So unless you fancy a chainsaw, pick from any of the others and we'll remove that choice for the rest."

I walk around the table, studying the weapons. I run a hand over a flamethrower and remember my introduction to life in this brave new world. I see Rage's eyes narrow–he wants a flamethrower–and I nearly pick it just to spite him. But I don't like fire.

"I'll take a spear," I decide, keeping it simple. The others make their choices. When we're ready, we carry our weapons through to another room, where leather suits and helmets are hanging up for us.

The trousers feel strange as I tug them on. I was never much into leather. I owned a couple of jackets in my time but no pants or shirts. The clothes feel tight on me, uncomfortable even with my less sensitive skin.

"Are these really necessary?" I grumble.

"They'll help protect you," Josh says. "You saw the way Rage was bitten. Leather *can* be penetrated, but not as easily as regular clothing. You'll be glad of it if a revived sinks their teeth into one of your legs or arms."

"But they can't infect us now, can they?" I frown. "We're zombies already."

"They can still hurt us, you idiot," Cathy snaps.

"A bite or a scratch stings like a bitch," Tiberius tells me. "And though moss will grow around it, you'll carry the wound for the rest of your life."

"Fair enough." I start to pull my T-shirt off, then pause. I don't have anything on underneath. I was never shy about my body, but I didn't go about flashing my tits to one and all. I glance around the room. The others are taking off their clothes and pulling on the leathers without any worries. The boys don't cover themselves, and Cathy doesn't either. They don't gape at one another or make suggestive comments, just get on with things, as if they're too grown-up to worry about a little nudity.

I shrug and pull off my T-shirt.

"Bloody hell!" Tiberius gasps and everybody looks up. At first I think he's staring at my boob and I prepare a hot retort. Then I realize it's the hole in my chest that caught his attention. "That's incredible."

"Not as incredible as your ginger hair," I mutter, but I feel oddly proud. The others can boast a cool variety of scars and bite marks, but nothing as outlandish as this.

Cathy comes closer and stares deep into the gaping hole. "That must have hurt like hell," she whispers.

"I can't remember," I lie, suppressing a shiver as I recall what it felt like when Tyler ripped my beating heart from between the shattered bones of my chest.

Cathy reaches out to put her hand in the hole, then pauses. "Do you mind?"

"Of course I bloody mind," I snort. "That'd be like me asking if I could stick my hand up your arse."

Everyone laughs and I tug on a leather shirt.

"It's an impressive wound," Cathy says grudgingly, then winks at me. "But the breast wasn't so hot."

"Get stuffed," I grunt, but we share a grin and I think she's finally forgiven me for cutting off her hair.

"Right," Josh says when we're ready, weapons in one hand, helmets in the other. "Most of you know the drill but I'll go through it again for Becky's sake. We're going to put you in with a group of reviveds. There's a speaker system inside each helmet. We'll be issuing orders as you go."

"Let's hope nobody breaks rank this time," Reilly huffs, looking pointedly at Rage.

"I've said sorry for that already," Rage groans. "I lost my head. It won't happen again. Promise."

"To start with, stand still," Josh goes on. "Let them mill around you. If they attack, defend yourself, but don't stir them up until we tell you. And when you do, follow orders as closely as you can, as long as you can, until things get chaotic. When we think the situation's getting out of hand, we'll drop the nets and bring proceedings to a close. Any questions?"

"What's the point of it all?" I ask.

"We're testing the reviveds," Josh says. "Their reactions, what they respond to, what they ignore, how much they remember on an instinctive level from their old lives. We'll also be checking if they show signs of revitalizing, but that's not the main goal of the experiment, since it happens so rarely."

"How far can we go?" I press. "Do we draw the line at dismembering them, killing them, what?"

"You can't kill them," Josh laughs. "They're already dead."

"You know what I mean. If we destroy their brains, we'll finish them off. That's killing in my book."

"Well it shouldn't be," Josh snaps, losing his smile. "Don't think of these as people. Not even animals. They're walking corpses, monsters who would rip apart everything we know and cherish. They slaughtered friends of yours, maybe family members too, and one of them even killed *you*. There should be no room in your heart for sympathy, not where these beasts are concerned."

"Tear them to pieces," Danny snarls. "They'd do even worse to you if they had the chance."

"Well said." Josh is beaming again. "Now, if you're all ready and willing, let's do some business."

Everyone cheers and roars like gladiators. Reilly opens a

door–not the one we entered by–and we pass along a short corridor, just us seven zom heads, leaving the soldiers behind.

We enter a bare room like the one I found myself in the first time I recovered my senses. White walls, lots of windows, soldiers and scientists crowded behind them.

Rage clomps to the middle of the room and the rest of us follow. We form a tight circle. I'm nervous and I can tell that the others are too. They've been looking forward to this–it breaks the monotony–but in the quiet moments before it kicks off, they tense and wonder what will happen if it goes wrong.

Each of us tests our weapon, flexes our muscles, prepares for battle. I start to wish I'd chosen something more substantial than a spear. I don't feel as protected as the others. I wish I could swap it for a chainsaw.

Then three doors click open at the same time, in three different walls. There's a short pause, flickering shadows, the smell of blood in the air. Then about thirty zombies slip into the room, spread out, shake their heads and fix their snarling, ravenous sights on us.

ELEVEN

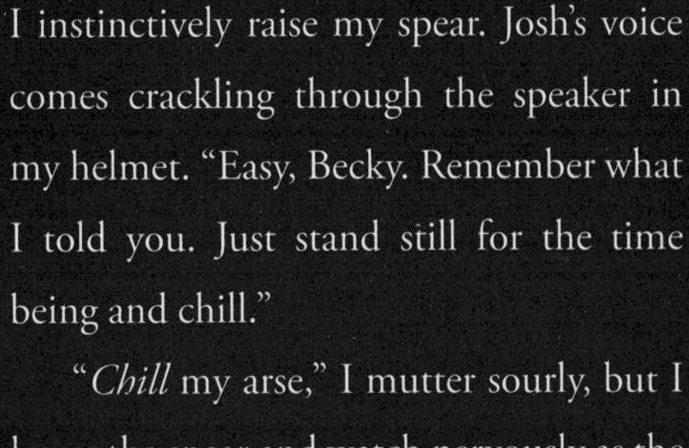

I instinctively raise my spear. Josh's voice comes crackling through the speaker in my helmet. "Easy, Becky. Remember what I told you. Just stand still for the time being and chill."

"*Chill* my arse," I mutter sourly, but I lower the spear and watch nervously as the zombies draw closer.

The first to come within striking distance is a woman. She's dressed in a filthy, tattered green blouse and a matching skirt. There are bite marks up and down her arms, as if her boyfriend got out of control when they were making out. Her eyes have a gray, cloudy film over them, like a blind person's, but by the way she focuses on me, I'm sure that she can see well enough.

The woman pauses in front of me and sniffs the air. Her mouth is open and her long, sharp teeth are bared. She makes a growling sound and I think she's getting ready to attack. My fingers tighten on the spear. But then she reels away to sniff the others.

I'm not sweating inside my helmet–I can't–but I feel hotter than normal. I keep a close eye on the zombies as they shuffle around, staring, sniffing, fingers twitching. I keep expecting one to realize that we're different, attack and set off the rest of their undead pack. But they don't. Because we're not *that* different, not in the most important way—like them, we're dead. Zombies clearly only have a taste for the living.

"That's good," Josh murmurs. "Let them get used to you."

"This is freaking me out," I croak.

"No," he says. "You've adjusted faster than the others did. You're the first to hold your nerve when making primary contact with reviveds. Even Rage lashed out the first time he was exposed."

That makes me feel smug. Of course it could be a load of bull and Josh might be saying it just to settle me down, but who can resist flattery like that? I treat myself to a self-indulgent chuckle, imagining Rage in a panic. I'll tease him about that later.

We hold our ground, letting the zombies move around freely. They don't have much interest in anything, not even each other. They creep in their own directions, swiveling to avoid collisions when they catch sight of one another but not communicating or cooperating in any clear way.

I start to feel sorry for them. They were real people once, with families, jobs, friends, hopes, dreams. What if some small part of them is still alive in there, if they can sense what they've become? How awful would that be?

"Okay," Josh says. "We're going to shake things up a bit. Raise your spear."

I hold it up as Josh instructs, then wave it threateningly at a passing zombie.

The zombie doesn't react.

"Do it again," Josh says. "But yell this time."

I roar at a different zombie—a man—and poke my spear at him, but he ignores me like the first one did.

The other zom heads make threatening gestures too, reacting to instructions. We must each have a separate guide, someone to direct us individually.

"Back up closer to the others," Josh says. "Form a tighter circle, so the reviveds can't pass between you."

I ease back as ordered, until my elbows brush against Danny's and Gokhan's. Danny has a chainsaw, Gokhan an ax.

"Exciting, innit?" Gokhan shouts, raising the visor of his helmet to grin at me.

The zombies close to us pause when they hear him shout and they stare at him, eyes wide and gray. "Yeah," Gokhan jeers. "You didn't expect me to talk, did you? You don't understand anything. We're gonna stomp your ugly arses. I'll cut your heads off with this ax and scoop out your brains. What do you think of that, eh?"

The zombies carry on walking, oblivious to the threat. Gokhan laughs and lowers his visor.

"Get ready for action," Josh whispers.

Rage has scorched the ceiling a couple of times, sending flames licking over the heads of the zombies. A couple of them cringed but didn't otherwise react. Now he lowers his hose, points the nozzle at a thin young woman and lets rip. Fire consumes her and she wheels away from him, screaming hoarsely, arms flapping, head shaking wildly.

The other reviveds come to a standstill. Their heads whip round and all eyes settle on Rage.

"Come on, you bastards," Rage growls.

As if in direct response to his challenge, they attack.

Instant chaos. Rage sprays the zombies with flames, and so does Tiberius, who has the other flamethrower. But they can't cover all angles and moments later the zombies are on us, digging at our stomachs with the bones sticking out of their fingers, gnashing at our faces, hissing and screeching.

I jab at a couple of my assailants, driving them back. The other zom heads are going wild. Cathy and Danny's chainsaws are alive and buzzing. Peder and Gokhan are chopping madly at the zombies, snickering hysterically.

Cathy digs the head of her chainsaw into a man's stomach and grinds it around. Blood and guts spray everywhere. The man falls away, screaming, a massive hole through his body where his middle should be. But that's not the end of him. Even though he's shrieking with agony, he crawls towards us, innards dribbling out and smearing the floor, driven to keep coming by a force beyond his control. His eyes are wild. Blood foams from his lips. He shudders and spasms like someone being electrocuted. But still he comes on.

"My go!" Peder cheers and chops at the man's neck until he severs it. With a sick laugh, he picks up the head by its hair and waves it around. The man's mouth is still opening and closing. His eyes still work. His arms still writhe on the now headless body and his legs kick out feebly at nothing.

Peder throws the head across the room and it bounces off a wall. The man's body somehow struggles to its feet and staggers around, arms flailing, trying to find his head. I'm appalled – if I had a heart, it would go out to the distressed zombie – but the others are having a ball.

"Can I go help him?" Danny yells gleefully. He must receive a positive answer because he breaks away and dashes across the room. Rage and Tiberius cover him, training their fire on the zombies who target him.

Danny grabs the headless body and hauls it over to where the head is lying. He picks up the severed head and sticks it on the neck, but back to front. With a ghoulish giggle, he returns to the ranks and restarts his chainsaw.

I stare with horror as the man swivels several times, trying to work out what's wrong. Finally his head falls off again. His body bends and his arms search for the missing head. Finding it, he puts it back in place, but the right way round this time. He holds the head in place by crooking an arm over it. With a snarl, he hurls himself back into the action and throws himself at me.

I'm frozen with shock, hardly able to believe the joy with which the zom heads have gone about their cruel business. Reacting instinctively when I'm attacked, I jab at the man's stomach, but of course there's nothing there, so my spear passes straight through the hole. Before I can pull it back, he's on me, eyes wide with crazy rage, teeth snapping together as he tries to chew through my helmet.

"Protect yourself!" Josh shouts.

I shove the man away, but he catches on the spear and doesn't fall. He bounces back towards me and his head collides with mine. His arm slips and his head falls to the floor, but the force of the collision cracks the glass in my visor. With a shriek of alarm, I push his body away, readjust my grip on my spear, then drive it down into the man's skull, all the way through his brain.

I lift the spear and the man's head rises into sight. His lips are trembling and he's making an awful choking noise. Blood drips from his neck and spatters my gloved hands. His eyes stare at me through the cracked lens of my visor. It might be my imagination, but I think I see fear in his expression.

"Cool!" Cathy exclaims, then sprays the head with flames. The stench of burning flesh and hair fills my nostrils and I gag. If I'd eaten anything recently, I'm sure I'd throw up, but my stomach is empty, so I only dry heave.

"Sod this!" I cry, and throw my spear away.

"Becky," Josh snaps. "What are you doing?"

Losing all control, I step away from the others and rip loose my helmet, freeing my face.

"Replace that!" Josh yells. "Get back in line!"

In answer I scream wordlessly, a monstrous howl. The world tilts crazily around me. I can't take this anymore. I want it to stop.

I clamp my hands over my ears and try to shut my eyes. When I remember that I can't, I scream again and grab the spear. I kick the flaming head off of it, then snap the shaft in two. I point the half with the tip at my eyes, determined to blind myself to this nightmarish spectacle, maybe even dig around, rip out my brain and finish the job that Tyler started all those months ago.

Rage knocks my arm aside. I bring it up to try again but he grabs my hand and forces it down, then wrestles the spear from my fingers and tosses it away.

I curse Rage and swing for him with my fists. Zombies crowd around and tear and snap at us. I feel bones scrape down the back of my exposed neck. I shriek madly and roar them on to success.

Rage swears and punches me. My nose pops and blood oozes out. I choke on it, shake my head, scream again.

Then nets start to come down on the zombies. Panels are ripped aside and soldiers fire through the gaps, shooting any revived who isn't caught. I try to pull free of Rage, to hurl myself into the hail of bullets, wanting to perish along with the zombies, feeling closer to them than to any of these warped, tormenting creeps. This is a savage, dreadful world, and I want out. I wish I'd never been brought back to life. I want to end it, stop it all, get off the moving train.

A net falls around me and I get tangled up. I lash out with both arms, trying to tear free, but the net only tightens further. With another scream, this time born of frustration at being cheated out of the death I crave, I fall to the floor and thrash around weakly, trapped in this living hell, forced to continue by the soldiers and scientists who gather round me once the zombies have all been killed or subdued. They stare at me coldly and listen to me shower them with abuse.

I'm still screaming when a man pushes through the others and crouches next to me. "Stop it, B," he says softly.

I ignore him, thinking it's Josh or Dr. Cerveris.

"Stop that," the man says again. When I don't, he grabs the netting around my head, ignoring the warning cries of the soldiers, and jerks my face towards his. "Look at me!" he barks.

I try to spit at him but my mouth is too dry.

"Look at me," the man says again, quieter this time, and

something in his tone makes me pause. It's not Josh or Dr. Cerveris, but his voice is familiar.

Suppressing the scream that was building at the back of my throat, I focus on the light brown face in front of me and gasp. *"Mr. Burke?"*

"Yes," he says, then grabs my gloved hand and squeezes reassuringly. "You can relax now. I'm here for you, B."

I'm so astonished, I can't say anything else, and I don't resist as two soldiers haul me to my feet, cut away the net from around my feet, and force me out of the room, Billy Burke – my favorite teacher from school – incredibly, impossibly, following close behind.

TWELVE

I'm in a small room, not much bigger than my cell. Sitting at a desk, arms cuffed behind my back, legs shackled to my chair. Still wearing the leathers. Staring at the table, jaw slack, thinking back to what happened with the zombies, the way I snapped. Wincing at the memory of the man's burning head, driving my spear through his brain, helping kill him.

Burke and Josh are sitting across from me, waiting, saying nothing. I listen to the hum and crackle of the building. I like it here, away from the zom heads, zombies, all that crap. I'd be happy if they never took me back.

The door opens and Dr. Cerveris steps in. He's seething. Glares at me as if I've insulted his mother. Sits with Burke and Josh on the other side of the table.

"Is she secure?" he snaps.

"Yes," Josh says.

"You're certain?"

"We don't take chances."

Dr. Cerveris sneers at me. "You're a very silly girl."

"Get stuffed," I snort, and he quivers indignantly. Before he can retort, I lock gazes with Burke. "What the hell are *you* doing here?"

"I'm a consultant," he says in a deadpan voice.

I laugh at the sheer absurdity of it. "What happened to being a teacher?"

He smiles thinly. "There isn't much call for teachers these days. Education has slipped down the list of priorities. That's what happens when you find yourself caught in the middle of a war with the living dead."

"Careful," Josh says warningly. "Don't forget the restrictions we discussed."

"Don't worry," Burke sighs. "I won't give away any of your precious secrets, though I don't see what you gain by withholding information from her." He runs a hand through his hair. It's grayer than it was six months ago. His eyes are bloodshot, dark bags underneath. He stinks of coffee.

"What was that about in there?" Burke asks me. "Why did you flip?"

"If you'd ever stuck a spear through someone's head, maybe you'd understand," I mutter.

"It didn't bother the others," Burke says.

"Well, it should," I snarl. "We were burning and hacking up *people*. When the hell did that become acceptable?"

"I told you before you went in," Josh growls. "They're not people. They're monsters."

"No, *we're* the monsters. They can't help themselves. We can." I face Burke again. "You remember Tyler Bayor?"

He has to think for a moment. "Tyler. Yes. He didn't make it."

"That's because I threw him to the zombies."

Burke raises an eyebrow and I quickly tell him about my dad coming to rescue me, yelling at me to throw Tyler to the undead when we needed to stall them, the way I obeyed.

"You tried to warn me," I finish sullenly. "You told me I was in danger of becoming a racist and it would end badly if I didn't change my ways. I didn't listen until it was too late. But I've thought a lot about it since I came back. I'm trying hard to be a better person in death than I was in life. I've been given a second chance, and I don't want to screw it up."

"That's admirable," Burke says without any hint of condescension. "But I don't see what it has to do with this."

"Your kind were all the same to my dad," I mumble. "Blacks, Arabs, Pakis." I catch myself and make a face. "*Pakistanis*. They were something less than us, not worthy of being treated as equals.

I knew he was wrong, but I never called him on it. I played along. And me throwing Tyler to the zombies was the result of that.

"The way Dad thought about different races... about *you*... the way I pretended to believe those things too..." I glance with shame at Mr. Burke, then with spite at Josh and Dr. Cerveris. "It's how you lot see zombies."

"It's hardly the same thing," Dr. Cerveris protests. "Racists hate for no valid reason, because of the color of a person's skin or their religious beliefs. Reviveds, on the other hand, are unnatural beasts, savage killers brought back to life by forces beyond our comprehension. They shouldn't exist. They've wreaked irreparable damage and will destroy the world completely if we don't dissect and study them and figure out what makes them tick."

"We experiment so that we can learn and understand," Josh says. "I know it might not seem that way. It could look like torture and execution to a neutral. But there are no neutrals here. It's us against them, with you and the other revitalizeds caught between. We use the zom heads because you can get closer to the reviveds than we can, test them in ways we can't. Your input might help restore control of this planet to the living. Zombies are dead. They can't be cured. Would you rather we let them run free and kill?"

"No," I scowl. "I understand why you have to stop them, why you lock them up, even why you execute them. But there must be other ways to experiment on them." I look pleadingly to Burke. "There *must* be."

"Of course there are," Burke says.

"Billy..." Josh growls.

Burke waves away the soldier's objection. "She's not a fool. You're right, B. It *is* cruel. It's inhuman. On a moral level it's unpardonable." He shrugs wearily. "But we're at war. That's not a great excuse, I know. I certainly wouldn't have let my students get away with it in class if they'd tried to use that argument to justify war crimes. But this is where we're at. I don't call the shots and I don't have the right to pass judgment. So I do what I can to help, even if it means going against everything I once believed in." He nods at Josh and Dr. Cerveris. "These gentlemen would appreciate it if you would too."

I shift uncomfortably. "It's wrong."

"Yes," Burke says. "But we're asking you to cooperate regardless."

"You were better than that once," I whisper.

Burke winces, looks away shamefully, doesn't respond.

"A racist zombie taking the moral high ground," Dr. Cerveris jeers.

"She's not a zombie," Burke snaps.

"Thanks to you," Josh says softly.

I frown. "What does that mean?"

Burke is looking at Josh, surprised. "I thought I wasn't supposed to mention that."

"You weren't," Josh says. "But if we tell her, maybe we can get through to her..."

Burke chuckles cynically. “When all else fails, try the truth.” He winks at me. “We don’t know why certain zombies revitalize. It’s a mystery. Based on all the studies we’ve conducted, it shouldn’t happen. The dead lose their senses. Their brains shut down and all traces of their old selves are lost. In damn near all of them, that loss is permanent, no way back.

“But a few of you defy the laws. You recover consciousness and carry on as you did when you were alive, for however long your bodies hold up.”

“Any idea how long that might be?” I interrupt.

Burke checks with Josh, who frowns, then shrugs. “Why not?” he says with just a hint of dark relish.

“We think–” Burke begins.

“It’s an imprecise science,” Dr. Cerveris cuts in coolly. “We have little evidence to back up our theories. But judging by what we’ve seen, and forecasting as accurately as we can, we anticipate an eighteen- to twenty-four-month life cycle for revitalized specimens.”

“You mean I’ll shut down and die for real within a couple of years?” I gasp.

“Maybe as little as a year,” Josh says. “You’ve been with us for more than six months already, remember.”

“But the revitalization process only kicked in a matter of weeks ago,” Dr. Cerveris reminds him. “We’re not sure if the time before that counts or not.”

"Wait a minute," I snap. "Are you saying that all of the zombies will be wiped out within the next two years?"

"Sadly, no," Dr. Cerveris replies. "Only the revitalizeds. The brains of the reviveds are stable, and from what we've seen, will remain so, at least in the near future. But when consciousness returns, the brain starts to operate differently. It conflicts with the demands of its undead body and begins to decompose. Unless we can find a way to counteract that–and so far we haven't had much opportunity to study the phenomenon–the prognosis is grim."

"So I've a couple of years max," I sigh.

"If they're right," Burke says. "They might not be."

"But we usually are," Dr. Cerveris smirks.

"That's not your main worry, though," Burke says.

I raise an eyebrow. "There's worse than being told I'll be worm fodder in a couple of years?"

Burke nods solemnly. "The first revitalizeds didn't last long. They were isolated once their guards noticed the change in them, but after a week or so, they reverted. Their brains flatlined and they went back to being mindless zombies. No one has ever recovered their mental faculties a second time."

"What changed?" I murmur.

"We found a way to prolong the revitalization," Dr. Cerveris says proudly.

"How?"

"Nutrients."

"You mean the gruel you've been feeding us keeps our brains going?"

"Yes. Without it, you would deteriorate rapidly."

I stare at the doctor, then Burke. "For a bunch of quacks who don't know why the dead reanimate or how some of us regain our senses, they seem to have figured out that part pretty quickly."

Burke smiles. "Good, B. You're thinking clearly, looking for answers behind the half-truths and lies. Go on. Take it further."

"I don't know if we need to tell her that much," Josh intercedes.

"We've guided her this far," Burke counters. "There's no harm in letting her go all the way."

I try to make sense of what I've been told, but I run into a brick wall. "It's no good," I tell Burke. "I don't know what you want me to work out."

"Think," Burke groans. "What's the one thing that zombies everywhere–from those you've seen in movies to those you saw at the school–go wild for? If you had a zombie locked up, and it was bellowing and wailing, how would you calm it down?"

"I don't..."

I stop, flashing on an image of the video footage that Josh showed me, of me bent over a boy, digging around inside his skull. In all the films I saw, all the comics I read, I never came across a zombie who didn't hunger for the juicy gray matter common to humans everywhere. The kind of gray matter, I realize with a sick jolt, that Reilly has been serving me every day.

Burke sees that I'm up to speed. He grins humorlessly, then says without emotion, "They've been feeding you human brains to keep you conscious. You need them to survive."

"So tell us again," Dr. Cerveris says smugly as I stare at them with revulsion and horror. "*Who's* the monster here?"

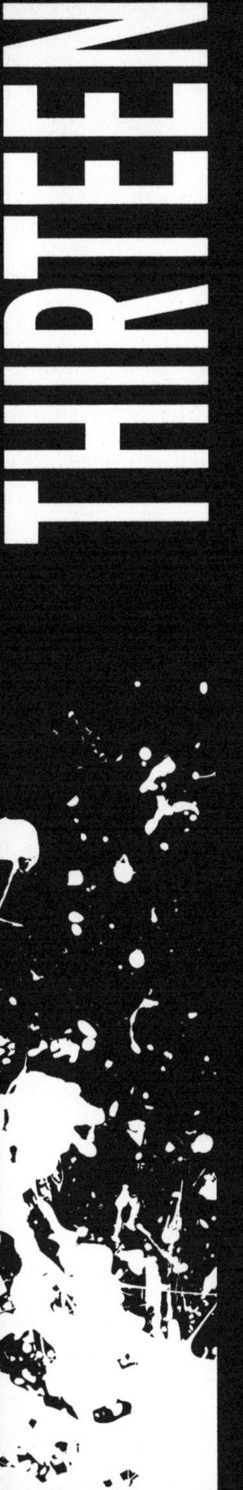

THIRTEEN

There's a long silence while I come to terms with what I've been told. This is certainly a meeting to remember. It's not every day that you find out you've got less than two years to live, and by the way, you've been feasting on human brains for the past month. But after my initial shock it doesn't take me long to get a handle on myself.

"Where do the brains come from?" I ask.

Burke says, "I told you — humans."

"I mean, are you killing people in order to feed us?"

"Don't be ridiculous," Dr. Cerveris snorts.

"The casualties have been horrendous," Josh explains. "We can't put an exact figure on how many people have been slaughtered, but in London alone we reckon it must run into the millions."

"That's not including the hundreds of thousands who have been turned," Dr. Cerveris points out. "Just those who were killed, whose heads were cracked open, so that they couldn't revive."

"We've mopped up a lot of the corpses," Josh continues. "Reviveds rarely clean out a skull—they almost always leave bits of brain behind. Ever since we realized what revitalizeds need, we've been collecting brain matter and storing it."

There's silence again. I stare at the wall above Burke's head. This wasn't how I saw my life going when I was at school. I didn't have any great career plans, but cannibalism was *very* far down my list of options.

I chuckle drily and lower my gaze. "You know what?" I grin crookedly. "Sod it. I always wanted to go on a TV show and eat things like bugs, snakes, roadkill. This is a dream come true. Bring it on. I'll eat whatever the hell you chuck at me." I rub my stomach slowly. "*Yum.*"

Burke smirks. "I told them you were a piece of work." He glances at Josh. "I bet you're glad now that you listened to me."

"We'll see," Josh mutters. "She hasn't agreed to cooperate yet."

I frown, thinking back a few minutes, then turn to Burke. "Josh said it was thanks to you that I wasn't still a zombie. What did he mean?"

"I was coming to that before you sidetracked me." Burke crosses his hands on the table and looks at me seriously. "Revitalizeds need brains to thrive. If we don't feed them, they regress. In most cases, the staff here let that happen."

I cock my head sideways. "Come again?"

"The percentage of reviveds who revitalize is minuscule," Dr. Cerveris says defensively. "But if you take a group of hundreds of thousands, even a fraction of a percent is significant."

"I figured there must be more of us," I say slowly, "that adults and younger kids were being held elsewhere."

"Of course," Dr. Cerveris says. "We keep a sample of all age groups, races, both sexes."

"A *sample,*" I repeat, knowing what that must mean but waiting for them to confirm it.

"They let most revitalizeds regress," Burke says. His gaze hasn't wavered. "They separate the conscious zombies, hold them in a cell, don't feed them, then return them to the general holding pens once they've–"

"– lost their bloody minds!" I roar. I try to jump to my feet but the chains around my ankles hold me in place.

"There are limits to the numbers we can maintain," Dr. Cerveris says calmly.

"Bullshit!" I retort. "You just don't want the hassle."

"We only need a few to study and help us with our experiments," Josh says. "What would we gain by keeping the others?"

"They can think!" I scream. "They're people. They have rights."

"Rights?" Josh sneers. "Only the living have rights, and they're not

alive, not really. You aren't either. You're a freak revived, nothing more, a threat to any normal person, never more than a few skipped feeds away from insane savagery. We keep you because we need you, but you have no rights. You lost those when you died and became a killer."

"Is that how you think too?" I ask Burke, trembling with rage.

"No," he says. "To me it's abhorrent."

"Then how can you work with them?" I snarl. "Why do you put up with this crap? Why not walk away, like anyone halfway human would?"

Burke shakes his head and doesn't reply.

"I wouldn't be so quick to criticize your old teacher if I were you," Dr. Cerveris says smoothly. "You'd be back stewing with the reviveds if it weren't for Billy Burke."

"We run a background check on every revitalized," Josh says. "We like to know who they are, where they came from. We gather as much information as we can before deciding how to process them."

"I bet that's so you can give priority to family members or people related to politicians or powerful businessmen," I sneer.

Josh shrugs. "I'd be lying if I said that wasn't a consideration, but that's the way the world has always worked. Nepotism is rampant everywhere. But if it's any consolation, very few revitalizeds fall into that bracket, so it's rare that someone is sacrificed at the expense of a minister's son or a billionaire's daughter."

"When they ran a check on you," Burke says, "they discovered your connection to me. I'm a consultant, like I told you. I've been working with the army, helping deal with undead children who are finding it hard to cope. Most are distraught at having lost family and friends. They don't all adjust as swiftly as you have."

"More's the pity," Dr. Cerveris murmurs. "Our lives would be a lot simpler if every revitalized were as cold and uncaring as Becky Smith."

I look at the doctor with contempt. "Screw you, numbnuts. I care. You don't understand me at all, do you?"

"That's why I've been kept busy," Burke says as Dr. Cerveris scowls at me. "I *do* understand, or at least I have a good idea. I never thought of it as a gift, being able to relate to teenagers, but it seems that talent is rarer than I believed. If it weren't for me and a few others, you guys would have been branded as cattle and treated the same way."

"I don't think we'd have gone quite that far," Josh smiles frostily. "Anyway, we realized you were one of Billy's ex-students, so we asked him if he wanted us to approve you for sustained revitalization."

"And you said yes." I flash my teeth at Burke in a mock smile. "Thanks. You're my hero."

"It wasn't as simple as that," Burke says quietly. "I had to pitch for you. I told them you were tough, smart, determined, that you'd be an asset."

"In short," Josh snaps, "he told us you'd fit in perfectly with the zom heads, that if we wanted someone to carry out harsh but essential tests on reviveds, you were our girl. That's why we spared you.

Otherwise..." He puts a finger to the side of his head, twirls it round and makes loony eyes at me.

"Nice to know you think so highly of me," I snarl at Burke.

"Would you rather I'd let you revert?" he asks gently. "Should I have abandoned you and left you to rot?"

I frown uncertainly. I can see where he's coming from, but still...

"You had no right to promise on my behalf," I mutter. "You shouldn't have told them I'd be willing to torture people–"

"Zombies," Josh slips in.

"– and kill them," I finish.

"I know," Burke says. "But I figured if they kept you alive, at least you'd have the chance to make that decision yourself. You're faced with a choice, B. It's not a welcome choice, and I honestly don't know how I'd react in your place, but it must be better than having no choice at all."

"And that choice is...?" I challenge him.

"Do what they ask and stay on as a zom head," he says evenly. "Or refuse to do their bidding and become a senseless zombie again."

"Not much of a choice, is it?" I huff.

"No," he admits. "But if you choose to defy them, at least you'll give up on consciousness willingly. The other way, you'd have simply regressed without any understanding of why it was happening to you."

"So I can become a vicious mercenary or a brain-dead cannibal. That's what you're telling me?"

"Boiled down to its basics, yes," Burke says.

Josh coughs politely. "I don't see any point in taking this conversation further. You know where you stand, Becky. It's time to decide. Will you help us or do we send you back to the pens?"

I stare at the three men, thinking hard. I'd like to say it's an easy choice, but it's not. I want to do the right thing and toss their offer of cooperation back into their ugly, cynical faces. I want to stand tall and proud like a hero, face true death willingly, without any regrets.

But at the same time I don't want to fade away and become a brainless member of the walking dead. They're going to carry out their experiments with or without me. Why not play along and cling to the semblance of life that I have? It wouldn't make any difference in the grand scheme of things.

When we did history at school and studied the Nazis, I was always scornful of the collaborators, those who morally objected to the cruelties but went along with them anyway, guards at death camps, doctors who were asked to experiment on live subjects, tailors who made clothes for soldiers, factory workers who provided them with guns. I thought they were cowards. There was no doubt in my mind that I'd have refused to help the Nazis just to save my neck.

Now I realize it's not that simple. If it's put to you plainly, cooperate or die, it's impossible not to have doubts. Maybe a saint would shake her head and refuse to consider the possibility of collusion, but I'm no saint. Hell, I'm not even halfway human.

But I've experienced firsthand the dreadful consequences of

meekly obeying people who are rotten to the core. Tyler's face flashes through my thoughts, as it does a dozen times a day, and I hear his cries again as the zombies bit into his flesh, see the pleading look in his eyes as he desperately begged me to save him. When I jumped at my dad's command and threw Tyler to the zombies, didn't I become a collaborator of sorts, as guilty as anyone who served the Nazis?

The man I helped kill today meant nothing to me. I didn't know him, wasn't connected to him, probably had little in common with him. Maybe he was a brute who deserved to die. But even if that was the case, he had a place in this world, a stake to existence, and I took that away from him. I vowed, after throwing Tyler to the wolves, that I'd never do it again. If I'm to honor that vow, I've got to treat everyone the same, not pick and choose those who count and those who don't. No collaboration, not if it costs me what little might be left of my soul.

"I won't do it," I moan, staring miserably at the table. "You're a pack of jackals and I won't join your sick, screwed-up cause, even if you kill me."

"Oh, we won't kill you," Dr. Cerveris says. He leans across the table and stares at me coldly. "We have a far more fitting punishment for obstinate hypocrites like you. *Nil by mouth.* This time next week, when your brain has turned to mush, you'll eat your own mother if we set her before you."

"And who knows," Josh purrs menacingly, in what I can only pray is nothing more than a nasty little dig, "maybe we will...."

FOURTEEN

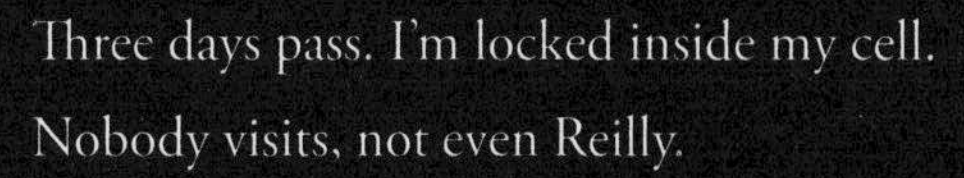

Three days pass. I'm locked inside my cell. Nobody visits, not even Reilly.

No food.

My stomach doesn't rumble. I don't feel hungry. But I'm twitchy. I find myself obsessing about the gray gunk that I used to be fed, craving more. I get shooting pains through my head and insides. Sometimes I have to double over and grit my teeth until the pain passes. My vision is getting worse, even though I keep adding the drops. Conversely, for some strange reason my sense of smell and hearing are improving. The noises of the complex often grind away at my brain until I have to clamp my hands over my ears to block them out.

Last night, when I was lying on my

bed, I blacked out for a while, the way I used to when I fell asleep. The next thing I knew I was on my feet, head butting the mirror. I'd smashed it to pieces but was still butting it, snarling softly.

I've tried to stay active since then, exercising, walking around my cell, doing push-ups and squats. I won't give in to fear. I *won't.* Let them starve me. I don't care. I'm not going to play their game. I'd rather die than become a killer.

Really? a small part of me whispers.

"Yeah," I tell it.

But my voice quivers and I'm not entirely sure that I can believe myself, that I can stay strong and true.

Working out. Keeping busy. Wanting to cling to consciousness for as long as I can, hoping that if I stay focused, it will help.

I've been thinking a lot about Mum and Dad. I'd managed to put thoughts of them on hold over the last few weeks, but Josh's threat about my mum has set me wondering again. I'm pretty sure they're not prisoners here–if Josh really had a card like that up his sleeve, he wouldn't have revealed it so casually–but are they squeezing out an existence in a similar complex? Were they killed? Turned into zombies? Or have they carried on as normal in a world not much different from the way it was on the day of the attacks?

By what I was told, millions of people were killed in London,

and hundreds of thousands were turned into zombies. But maybe Josh and the doctor were lying, feeding me misinformation to make me think the situation is worse than it really is.

As I'm driving myself mad thinking about the possibilities, the door suddenly slides open and Josh and Reilly stomp into my room. They both look impassive. I was doing squats but I stop and stand. Stare at the pair of them defiantly.

"I thought you might have had a change of heart," Josh says. The sound of his voice makes me wince, it's so loud.

"You forgot," I sneer, and pull up my T-shirt to expose the hole in my chest. "I don't have a heart."

Josh sighs. "I'm not enjoying this, Becky. I can rustle up some gruel for you in a matter of minutes if you give me the word."

"I can give you two words," I tell him. "The second is *off*. Can you guess the first?"

Josh shakes his head and laughs—to my sensitive ears, it's like a jackhammer. "I really hope you relent and come to see things our way," he says. "You and I could be great friends if you cut yourself a little slack."

"I'd cut my own throat before I'd claim you as a friend," I grunt.

Josh gasps theatrically, then nods at Reilly. "Take her through."

"Where?" I ask, tensing, thinking this is it, they're taking me back to the pens to dump me with the other zombies.

"Zom HQ," Reilly says, and holds up a pair of handcuffs. "I'm going to have to ask you to wear these on the way there and back."

"What if I don't want to?"

"I have orders to force you if necessary," he says.

"I don't mean about the cuffs," I snort. "Zom HQ—I don't want to go."

"Aren't you lonely?" Reilly asks. He's speaking more softly than usual. I think he knows that noises hurt me.

"No," I lie. "Even if I was, I'd rather suffer loneliness than sit with that shower of vipers. I've no friends there. They can all go hang."

"Even Mark? He wasn't involved with any of the experiments."

I shrug. "He wants to be."

"That's because he hasn't seen what they get up to." Reilly jangles the cuffs. "It's not an option, B. They're determined to send you there. I don't want to hurt you, but if you leave me no choice..."

I roll my eyes and glare at the smiling Josh. "All right. I'll come peacefully. Give me the bloody cuffs."

The zom heads look astonished when I walk in. They also look unhappy to see me. It's a good thing I wasn't expecting a warm welcome.

"What's she doing back here?" Tiberius shouts at Reilly as he unlocks my cuffs.

"I know you've been missing her, so I brought her along to cheer you all up," Reilly deadpans, then exits.

Rage squares up to me as I head towards my regular couch.

"What was all that crap about when we were experimenting on the zombies?" he growls.

"You might call it an experiment," I spit. "I call it torture and murder."

"You can't kill zombies," Rage says, looking genuinely surprised.

"Yeah, I know, they're already dead," I sneer. "Why don't you change the track? I've heard that one too many times. It's the regular excuse round here to do whatever the hell you want."

"But they *are* dead," Cathy protests. "It doesn't matter what happens to them."

"You're dead too," I remind her.

"That's different," she growls. "*We're* different."

"Yeah, but for how long?" I sniff.

Rage squints at me. "What's that mean?"

I consider telling them what I've learned, about how we regress if we don't feed, that we're kept conscious purely to serve the whims of Dr. Cerveris and his mob, who can take our minds away from us anytime they please. But I don't think they'd thank me for enlightening them. Treat me to a beating, more likely, for being the bearer of bad news.

"Just leave me alone," I mutter, shouldering my way past Rage.

"She thinks she's better than us," Tiberius jeers. "She probably wants to spread joy and peace among the zombies. Are we savages, *Becky*? Should we be put down like rabid dogs?"

I ignore him, grab a file and set to work on my teeth—I wasn't allowed a file in the cell, so they've sprouted. The others toss a few insults my way but ease up when I don't bite back. I'm glad when they stop talking. It's as noisy in here as it was in my cell, but I can deal with that. Their raised voices, on the other hand, strike me like punches.

Mark slides over after a while and grins weakly. "They told me what happened," he whispers.

"And you think I'm a fool," I snap, laying the file aside. "You think I should have gone along with the rest of them, hacked off limbs, burned people alive—or burned them *dead*, or however the hell you want to phrase it."

Mark shrugs. "I can't see what the fuss is, but I wasn't there. I've never been there. I don't know what goes on, so I can't judge." He slumps beside me. "To be honest, I think anything would be better than my checkups. They're operating on me more and more. They're worried about my organs, but I don't know why. I don't feel any different."

Mark rubs his eyes and I'm stunned to see his fingers come away wet.

"I thought all of our tear ducts had dried up," I murmur, grabbing his gloved hand and studying the moisture suspiciously.

"They've given me new drops," he explains. "A side effect is that I produce liquid that looks like tears. They say my eyes will dry up completely without the new drops, that I'll go blind." He sighs unhappily.

"Sorry," I mumble. "That must be horrible."

He nods. "But they're hopeful the drops will work. And it's nice having wet eyes again. They used to sting before."

My eyes don't really pain me, but I guess we're all different.

Mark says the zom heads have been in a foul mood since they returned from the terminated experiment.

"They snap at me all the time, but at each other too. They won't admit it, but I think they're ashamed as well as angry. When you refused to harm the zombies, it made them think about how willingly they've gone along with everything. It was just the way things were. Nobody thought they had a choice, or that there was anything wrong with what they were doing. Now they've started to question what they've done."

"And they're blaming me for that," I snicker. "Nobody likes a smartarse who shakes things up. The world's a lot simpler if you don't think too much about it. I'd be mad too in their shoes. I didn't want to rock the boat. I just couldn't take it. I can't see the reviveds as monsters. They're still people in my eyes."

Mark gives my arm a squeeze. "Don't worry," he says. "They'll forgive you. Everyone's grumpy because of the diet, but once they give us back our regular rations, I'm sure—"

"What are you talking about?" I cut in sharply.

"They stopped feeding us a couple of days ago," he says, surprised by my tone.

"You mean after the others came back from the experiment?" I press.

"Yeah. They fed us the first day, same as normal, but nothing since."

I curse loudly and everyone looks at me. I start to get to my feet, to tell them of my suspicions, then pause and sit down again.

I might be wrong. Best not to say anything until I'm certain. I don't want to stir them up if there's no real reason for it.

So I keep my own counsel and sit out the shift, the hours dragging even slower than usual. When Reilly comes and takes us away, one by one, like he always does, I wait until he's leading me back to my cell, then grunt my question at him without looking around. "Are the others being starved because of what I did?"

"Yes," he says without hesitation. "It was Dr. Cerveris's idea. I don't like it, but my vote doesn't carry much weight round here."

"My fading eyesight... my improving sense of smell and hearing... that's part of the regression?"

"Yes," he says. "Reviveds rely on their nostrils and ears more than their eyes. The others haven't been denied food quite as long as you have, so they haven't deteriorated as much as you. But they'll start to notice a significant change within the next day or two."

"How long can we go without food before we turn completely?" I ask.

"It varies from one revitalized to another," he says evenly. "But nobody's ever lasted more than a week."

"Are the doctors serious about this? It's not a bluff?"

"Dr. Cerveris doesn't bluff," Reilly says with what sounds like a genuine sigh. "He doesn't need to. There are other revitalizeds he can turn to."

"So if I refuse to cooperate…"

I falter, so Reilly finishes the sentence for me. "…then they'll let Mark and all the other zom heads starve and turn back into brain-dead zombies."

FIFTEEN

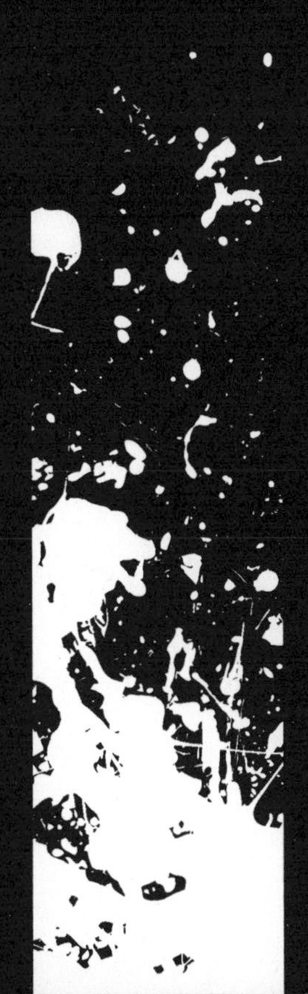

I spend my time in isolation trying to decide whether or not to tell the others about the threat we face. It should be a straightforward call—they have a right to know. But I'm worried about how they'll react. They kill reviveds because they see them as monsters. If I told them that we need to eat brains to survive, and that we're being denied the gruel because of my refusal to play ball with Dr. Cerveris and Josh, they might rip me to pieces. Literally.

I've seen them do it to others. Killing gives them a buzz, and it's bull when they say that they only do it because they have to. There's a good chance they'll slaughter me if I tell them the truth, in the hope that Dr. Cerveris will restore their rations if I'm removed from the equation. A lot of normal people would sacrifice me in a situation like this, so I can't expect too much compassion from a pack of semiliving beasts.

Then again, maybe they deserve the benefit of the doubt. It's wrong to let them perish in ignorance. And if they kill me, what of it? I'll be brain-dead in a couple of days anyway. Why drag the rest of them down with me?

"Because they're bastards," I mutter, and brood about it some more.

Everyone's sour as stale yogurt the next day. The lack of *nutrients* is kicking in big-time. The zom heads are wincing at noises, groaning as hunger pangs shoot through them. They can't understand why they're being denied the gray gloop or why they feel as rough as they do.

"We must have done something wrong," Tiberius insists as they knock the issue back and forth.

"Nah," Gokhan says. "It's a test, innit? They want to see what we do when we get hungry."

"I'll rip Reilly's head off," Peder growls. "That'll show them what *I* do."

"It isn't Reilly's fault," Danny says. "He's not enjoying this. It's bloody Josh who's behind it."

"No it's not," Cathy shouts, then makes a face and lowers her voice. "It's Dr. Cerveris. Josh doesn't have any say in how they test us. It's the scientists who decide those things. I'll ask Josh what's going on the next time I see him."

"Oh, I'm sure he'll tell *you*," Tiberius simpers. "You mean so much to him."

Cathy flips him the finger, then glares at Rage. He's the calmest of everyone, watching an old episode of some American sitcom set in a bar, chuckling softly at the punch lines.

"I don't know why you're so happy," Cathy snarls. "You're part of this too. You'll starve with the rest of us, no matter how many arses you kiss."

"Chill, baby," Rage sniffs. "The Turk's right. They're testing us. Once they've compiled enough data, they'll feed us again. They need us. We're their blue-eyed darlings."

"Maybe they're feeding you on the sly," Danny challenges him. "Maybe that's why you don't seem bothered."

"Believe what you want," Rage shrugs.

"You never say a bad word against them, do you?" Peder spits. "You're a right muppet."

"I relish the easy life," Rage counters. "If we scratch their backs they'll scratch ours. You don't win any prizes for rubbing against the grain. I do what they tell me, treat them with respect and reap the rewards."

"Do you call being starved a reward?" Mark asks.

"Shut it, Worm," Rage snaps, then carries on talking to Peder as if he were the one who had asked the question. "They've got to treat me the same as everybody else when they're running a test, stands to reason. But in the normal run of things, by keeping them sweet, I get anything I ask for, films, games, magazines, even girls if I wanted."

Danny laughs out loud, ignoring the others as they moan and slam their hands over their ears. "*Girls?*" he shrieks. "What the hell would you want with those? We're all dead down below. We can't do anything with girls except look."

"That's why I said *if* I wanted," Rage replies smoothly.

Mark is frowning and staring at his groin. This is news to me. I hadn't realized the boys were impotent, though now that I consider it, it makes sense—no blood flow to stir their sleeping soldiers. If the situation weren't so dire, I'd have a good old chuckle about it. But they've more important things to worry about than dodgy machinery in their boxer shorts. And on impulse, having listened to them waffle on about this all day without saying a word, I suddenly decide to solve the mystery for them.

"It's because of me. They're starving you because I won't torture the reviveds. And they're not gonna stop until..."

I draw to a halt. Everyone is staring at me, even Rage, who doesn't look so cocky anymore.

"Go on," Tiberius says stiffly.

"The gray junk they've been feeding us is human brains."

"We know," Tiberius says.

"You *know*?" I exclaim.

He shrugs. "It's obvious. We figured that out months ago. Zombies eat brains, everyone knows that."

"You never told me," I huff.

"We didn't know that we needed to," Tiberius sneers. "How thick are you?"

"Enough of that," Rage snaps, getting to his feet. He looks uneasy. "Finish what you were going to say."

"We need the brains to stay conscious," I mutter. "Without regular feeds we'll lose our senses and become reviveds again. And if we do, we can't recover, we'll be stuck like that forever."

Rage stares at me coldly. Everybody else is gaping too.

"They told you this?" Cathy asks.

"Yeah."

"And you said nothing?" Her voice rises. "You let them starve us, knowing what would happen, not saying a word?"

"I'm telling you now."

"You bitch!" she shrieks. "That's the first thing you should have–"

"I'm calling Reilly," Rage says heavily. "I'm gonna tell him that you've agreed to do whatever they ask. Then we're gonna go tear some zombies to shreds and you'll hack them up, burn them, slice them into little pieces, and that will be that."

"No," I whisper. "They're people. I won't do it."

"You bloody well will," Rage snarls, stomping towards me.

I stand and face his challenge, hands by my sides. I don't flinch when he makes a fist and holds it threateningly in front of my face.

"A beating won't change my mind," I tell him. "I've been in plenty of fights, taken more than my fair share of thrashings. I took them at home too—my dad was handy with his fists, knocked me and Mum around all the time. You can smash me to a pulp, break my arms, snap my fingers, rip my ears off. It won't matter. I won't give in."

"I'll kill you," Rage croaks.

"Maybe," I concede. "I'll fight back, and I think Josh will stop you before it gets that far, but if you're tough enough and fast enough, maybe you can finish me off before they intervene."

"Do it," Danny says flatly, stepping up beside Rage. "I'll help."

"Me too," Gokhan growls.

"What about the rest of you?" Rage barks.

"I dunno," Peder says, looking worried. "She's not like the other zombies that we kill. She's one of us."

"But she won't be if they don't feed her," Cathy says, then frowns. "How long before we change?" she asks me.

"No one can last more than a week without being fed, so a few days at most."

Cathy's face hardens. "Kill her. If she's going to revert anyway, we should off her while we can. Otherwise we'll all turn into reviveds."

"No," Mark moans. "We can't do this. It's not right. It's murder."

"But if it's us or her..." Rage says heavily.

Tiberius pushes past Rage and glares at me. I wait for him to condemn me too, but to my surprise he comes out with something bizarre. "I was named after Captain Kirk in *Star Trek*."

Everyone stares.

"I tell people I was named after the river in Rome, but really it was after Kirk. His full name was James Tiberius Kirk. My mum and dad loved *Star Trek*. They made me watch it all the time when I was growing up. Except they didn't have to make me—I loved it as much as they did. Kirk was my hero."

"Is this going somewhere, or have you lost your marbles?" Danny huffs.

"Kirk always stood up for the underdog," Tiberius says. "Every week, him and his crew risked their lives to save others. They killed the bad guys when they had to, but they never killed innocents, not even to save themselves."

"That was just a TV show," Cathy jeers.

Tiberius nods. "I know. But it was *right*. I watched Kirk, Bones and the rest of them, and I knew they were doing the right thing. I was sure I'd do the same thing in their position. I used to hope that one day something dangerous would happen to me, so that I could prove how brave and loyal and *human* I was.

"Reviveds are different," Tiberius says, facing Rage. "I don't think Kirk would have fought for a load of mindless, walking corpses. But Peder's right—B's one of us. If we kill her, we really will be monsters. And I'm not prepared to let that happen. I'll fight with her if I have to, die with her if it comes to that."

Rage holds Tiberius's gaze, deliberating. The others await his verdict. Finally he grunts and looks aside.

"We'll think it through some more," he mutters. "I'll have a chat with Reilly, see if there's another way to sort this out. But if there isn't... well, we'll discuss that tomorrow. See how we all feel about it then."

Rage returns to his couch and the others disperse, shooting me dark looks. Mark and Tiberius remain. Mark's trembling. Tiberius is stiff as a mannequin.

"Thanks," I mutter, knowing the word isn't enough.

"Screw you," Tiberius says. "You're crazy, making a stand like this. Go away and have a rethink, then start cutting up zombies like you're told. Because if you don't, I doubt I can save you next time." He glances at me and I've never seen such an expression before, torn between pride and self-loathing. "I don't even know if I'll try."

Then he storms off and Mark slips away too, leaving me alone, hated, a pariah. But, against all the odds, they didn't kill me. I'm still alive.

But not, I suspect, for long.

SIXTEEN

In my cell, lying on the bed. The pain is worse than ever. My head throbs and my fingers tremble wildly. I had the dry heaves a while ago, my body in revolt. I tried exercising and keeping active, but now it hurts too much when I move. I think I'm close to the end. All I want is to shut my eyes and drift off. I don't care if I never regain consciousness.

"I'm sorry," I whimper, but I don't know if I'm apologizing to the ghost of Tyler Bayor for killing him, my mum for letting Dad beat her up for so many years and not reporting him, myself for giving up, or somebody else. I'm not at my sharpest at the moment.

There's a screeching sound from the corridor and I jam my hands over my ears, groaning weakly. The noises have increased over the last few minutes. I've been hearing all sorts of things, explosions, tearing metal, screams. I know they aren't real. It's just my brain cascading out of control, warping ordinary sounds out of recognition.

Is this how it is all the time for regular zombies? Is that why they moan so much? I try to imagine a lifetime of this crazy noise, shaking from the hunger, nearly blind, scouring the ruins of the world in search of brains. Some life! Maybe I should end it all before I regress.

I lower my hands and stare at the sharp bones sticking out of my fingertips. It would be difficult, but I'm sure I could crack open my skull and scoop out enough of my brain to put myself out of my misery. It would be a gruesome way to die, but wouldn't it be better than shuffling around as a lost, tormented soul for the rest of my wretched years?

As I'm staring at my fingers, trying to work up the courage to end it all, the door to my room slides open. The sounds outside amplify immediately and I wince. I glance up from my hands, expecting Reilly, or maybe Dr. Cerveris and Josh. But whoever it is, he's standing in the corridor, not showing his face. I can see his shadow, but that's all.

"Don't be shy," I growl. "Come on in and have a good look."

The man giggles. It's a strange, jangly sound. It makes me grit my teeth. I start to sit up angrily. Then the man steps inside and I sink back with confusion and disgust.

It's a clown, but no clown that you'd ever see in a circus, not unless it was a circus in hell.

He's dressed in a pinstripe suit, but with colorful patches stitched into it in lots of different places. There are plenty of bloodstains too.

A severed face hangs from either shoulder. The faces have been skinned from the bone. I think one came from a woman and the other from a man, but it's hard to be sure.

Lengths of gut are wound around both his arms, long strands of intestines, glistening and dripping. Along his legs several ears have been pinned to the fabric of his trousers.

He's wearing a pair of oversized red shoes, a small skull sticking out of the end of each. They could be the skulls of some breed of monkey, but I don't think they are. I think the skulls came from human babies.

The clown's hair has been sourced from a variety of heads. There are all sorts of locks, every type of color, shade and length, stuck to his skull. No... not stuck. As he comes closer and giggles again, he bends slightly and I see that the clumps of hair are stapled to his scalp. There are dried bloodstains around many of them, and fresh blood flows from a few.

The clown has a painted white face, but that's the only traditional touch. The flesh around his eyes has been carved away and filled in with what looks like soot. A pair of *v*-shaped channels run from beneath either eye to just above his lips, which have been painted a dark blue color. The channels have been gouged out of his cheeks and the exposed bone has been dyed bright pink. Instead of the usual red ball over his nose, he's somehow attached a human eye to it. Little red stars have been dotted over it.

I do nothing as the surreal clown advances. I'm frozen in place. I'm praying that this is an illusion, a product of my fevered brain. But he doesn't look like a dream figure. By all rights he shouldn't belong to this world, but he certainly seems at home in it.

The clown hops from foot to foot, performing a strange little shuffle, still giggling, drawing closer. Now I spot a button on his chest, round and colorful, the sort a child might paint. Daubed on the button, in very ragged handwriting, is what I assume is his name.

Mr. Dowling.

He reaches the foot of my bed and beams at me, lips closed, eyes wide, looking crazier and more menacing than anything I've ever seen. His eyes continually twitch from one side of their sockets to the other. His skin is wriggling, as if insects are burrowing beneath the flesh, close to the surface.

I want to kick out at the nightmarish clown, or slide past him and race from the cell. But I can't move. It's like I'm locked down tight. I can't even whine.

The clown reaches out and slowly strokes my right cheek. His fingers are long and thin. Much of the flesh has been sliced away from them. I glimpse bones through a mishmash of exposed veins

MR

and arteries. He's not a zombie—he has normal-looking nails, and I can feel his pulse through the touch of his fingers—so I can't understand how he tolerates these open, seeping wounds.

Withdrawing his hand, the clown—*Mr. Dowling*—leans over until his face is in front of mine. His eyes steady for a moment and he looks straight at me. Only it's more like he's looking through me. I feel as if he's reading my thoughts, stripping my mind bare, unraveling all of my secrets.

The clown's smile spreads. His eyes start dancing again. He opens his mouth.

Spiders fall from his blue lips, a rain of arachnids, small and scuttly. Hundreds of legs scrape my face as they pour upon me, over my eyes, into my mouth, up my nose.

With a scream of shock and terror, I snap back to life, hurl myself from the bed and roll across the floor, swiping spiders from my face, mashing them to pieces with the heels of my hands, spitting them out, picking them from my eyes, screaming over and over. I never thought of myself as an arachnophobe. Then again, I've never been covered with spiders until tonight.

I shake my head and wipe my hands across my face and scalp, brushing the last of the spiders away. Some scurry across the floor, seeking the shelter of the shadows under the bed. I poke the bone of my little finger into my right ear, then my left, as carefully as I can, not wanting to rupture the drums within. Then I explore slowly with my fingers.

They're gone.

With a shudder, I stand, squash a few more of the spiders underfoot and turn to face the otherworldly clown.

He isn't there. If he was real in the first place—and I wouldn't think that he was if not for the spiders—he slipped out while I wasn't looking.

And he left the door open.

Still shaking, I glance around my cell to make sure he's not lurking, waiting to pounce on me from behind when I think I'm safe. Once I'm convinced that he really has gone, I call out shakily, "Hello?"

There's no answer, but the noises outside are louder than ever, the screams especially. I no longer think that they're the product of my skewed senses.

Steeling myself against every sort of imaginable horror, I edge closer to the open doorway. I keep thinking that it will slam shut, but it doesn't, and seconds later I ease out of my cell, into the corridor and the middle of a blood-red storm.

SEVENTEEN

Soldiers are battling with zombies at the end of the corridor. A small group of humans, no more than four or five, against a dozen or more of the living dead. The soldiers have guns and are firing openly on their enemies, but unless the bullets strike their heads and rip the zombies' brains apart, they don't do any real damage. And the zombies aren't giving the soldiers the time or space to squeeze in many clear headshots.

My first instinct is to try to help the soldiers. It doesn't matter that they've been keeping me captive, or that they've been deliberately starving me for the last few days. I feel compelled to help the living.

The zombies have the soldiers surrounded. I start towards them, shouting,

trying to distract the undead killers. I'm not sure how I plan to help the humans, but at least I can fight off the zombies without fear of being infected. Maybe I can buy the soldiers time to retreat to safety.

But the reviveds put an early end to my half-formed plans. They press in close, dig in teeth and fingers, and it's all over before I hit the scene. They leave the humans before they fully turn, somehow knowing they've done enough.

The soldiers writhe on the ground and scream for help or mercy, but there's nothing anyone can do for them now. One puts a gun to his head and ends the nightmare before it can claim him. The others suffer on.

The zombies bunch together in front of me and sniff the air, pressing forward dangerously. I remember what happened during the experiment. The reviveds don't react to zom heads unless we attack them. It's hard, but I force myself to stand calmly as they circle me, fingers flexing, nostrils dilated.

They decide I'm one of them, lose interest in me and press on, moving with purpose. Soon I'm left with the soldiers, who are all vomiting and transforming. I can hear bones forcing their way out through fingers and toes, teeth thickening and lengthening. Turning my back on the doomed, screaming men, I make for zom HQ, hoping to find answers or safety there.

It's the first time I've been able to patrol the corridors by myself. Under normal circumstances I wouldn't get very far, but virtually all of the doors are open. The security system has either crashed or been hacked. There's nothing to hold me back. But that means there's nothing to hold back the zombies either. Or that grisly clown. Mr. Dowling could be lurking in any of the rooms that I pass or around any of the corners that I come to.

But there's no sign of the clown. I scope lots of zombies, and a few soldiers and scientists running for their lives, but that's all.

I'm close to zom HQ when a Klaxon starts to wail. The high-pitched sound is torturous and I collapse to my knees, choking with pain. Clasping my hands over my ears doesn't help. I feel like my head is about to split. I see zombies falling like ninepins, moaning and convulsing. It looks like the revolt has been quashed. Some bright spark has come to the rescue. It's probably for the best. As much as I hate the crew here for what they've done to me, I don't want to see them all slaughtered. I'll just wait, ride out the pain as best I can, and put up no resistance when they come to take me back to my...

The Klaxon dies away as swiftly as it blared into life. The zombies rise and shake their heads. They snarl accusingly at the ceiling, then press on in search of fresh victims, back in business, as hungry as ever.

I stagger on until I find zom HQ, but the door here is closed and doesn't open when I push. I pound on it and roar out names. "Rage! Reilly! Tiberius!" But nothing happens.

I'm not sure what to do now. I back away from the door, staring at it sullenly. An undead woman with one arm staggers past. She stops and turns, eyes widening with delight, lips splitting into an eager smile. Then a bullet rips through her forehead and tears her brain to shreds. She collapses with a soft wheezing noise.

I glance over my shoulder and spot Reilly and Dr. Cerveris jogging towards me. Gokhan, Peder and Cathy are with them. Reilly looks scared but in control. Dr. Cerveris just looks furious.

"How did you get out of your cell?" the doctor snaps as they draw level.

"The clown opened my door."

Everyone gapes at me.

"What bloody clown?" Reilly grunts.

"Mr. Dowling." I look around. "Nobody else saw him?"

"She's started to hallucinate," Dr. Cerveris huffs. "That's common among revitalizeds in the final stages of consciousness. We should leave her. She could regress at any time."

"They're all in bad shape," Reilly says, pointing to the others, who are shaking and dizzy-looking. "If we're going to try to save the rest, we might as well save B too."

"Very well," Dr. Cerveris mutters. "But if I give the command, blow her brains out and don't stop to think about it."

The doctor steps forward, presses his fingers to the panel on the zom HQ door, then puts an eye up to the retinal scanner. The door slides open and he looks inside. "Nobody home," he says, closing the door again.

"Why don't we hole up in there?" Peder asks. "The zombies couldn't get in if we shut the door behind us."

"Of course they could," Dr. Cerveris barks. "Members of staff have been turned. We know from past tests that certain operational memories remain among reviveds. Some of the soldiers and medics might recall what they need to do to open locked doors, and if they had clearance when they were alive, they still have it now."

"So what are we going to do?" I growl. "Run around like slasher-movie fodder until the zombies get us?"

"First we fetch the others," Reilly says as we pad down the corridor, following the animated Dr. Cerveris. "Then we lock ourselves into a room that requires a digital code. The reviveds won't be able to recall a string of numbers—their memories aren't *that* strong."

"How come you're bothering with us?" Cathy asks as we run. "Did Josh tell you to help us?"

"I haven't seen him," Reilly says. "I don't know if he's still alive. But it's our job to protect you. We're under attack. An outside crew has disabled our system and freed the reviveds, and their forces are still active. I thought we were safe when the Klaxon kicked in, but obviously they got to that too. I don't think they're interested in the reviveds–they can find more of them anywhere–so they must be after you guys."

"I've put too much work into this project to see it hijacked now," Dr. Cerveris says petulantly. "Once we've run off these invaders, I'll track down whoever was responsible for the attack and flay their flesh from their hides."

"So you aren't helping us out of humanitarian concern?" I jeer.

"Of course not," Dr. Cerveris says. "You aren't human."

I shake my head admiringly. He might be a son of a bitch, but at least he stays true to himself, even during a crisis.

We pick up Tiberius from his cell–it's quiet down his corridor and he had no idea that anything was amiss–then push on. A couple of corners later, we run into a pair of reviveds. They go wild when they catch the scent of Reilly and Dr. Cerveris. They hurl themselves at the humans. Reilly fires but misses. Before the zombies can take him, we wrestle them to the ground and hold them there while Reilly takes aim and shoots.

I hate doing this, helping him kill, but we have no choice. It's Reilly and Dr. Cerveris or the reviveds. And while my sympathies should lie with the zombies who've been imprisoned and maltreated, I can't stop thinking of myself as one of the living.

Mark's cell is next on our route. The door's open but he's cowering inside, hunched over in a corner, tears streaming down his face. (Those new drops are miraculous. Even with everything else that's going on, I feel a stab of jealousy and wonder why the rest of us have been denied them.)

"Mark!" Reilly barks. "Get your arse in gear. We're moving out."

Mark looks up and shakes his head. He opens his mouth to say something, but nothing emerges.

"What's wrong?" I ask, stepping towards him.

"Leave the little worm," Cathy grunts.

"Yeah," Gokhan sneers. "He's acting like a baby, eh?"

"He's coming with us," Dr. Cerveris says with unusual warmth.

He shoves past me and crouches by Mark's side. "Come on, Mark. We have to get out of here. We're going to take you to a safe place."

Mark stares at the scientist. A shadow flickers across his eyes and for a moment it looks to me as if he blinked. But of course that's impossible. The drops are good, but nothing can be *that* good, not for a zom head with paralyzed eyelids.

"Is he out there?" Mark whimpers, his gaze shooting towards the open doorway.

"Who?" Dr. Cerveris frowns.

Mark's gloved right hand is twitching by his side, fingers drumming the floor. But when I steal a closer look, I realize he isn't drumming—he's *squashing*. There are lots of dark smudges on either side of him. They could be ink blots, but I know that they're not.

They're smeared spiders.

"You saw the clown," I say, and Mark's eyes lock on mine.

"You saw him too?" he gasps.

I nod heavily. "Mr. Dowling."

"The button," Mark croaks.

It wasn't a hallucination. I'd started to doubt myself, but now I know for sure that my giggling visitor was real. There's no time to wonder at it, though. We have to get out of here and find sanctuary.

"Come on." I take Mark's hand and haul him to his feet. "We need to get away before the clown comes back."

That puts a rocket under Mark's arse and he bounces away from me and is first out the door.

EIGHTEEN

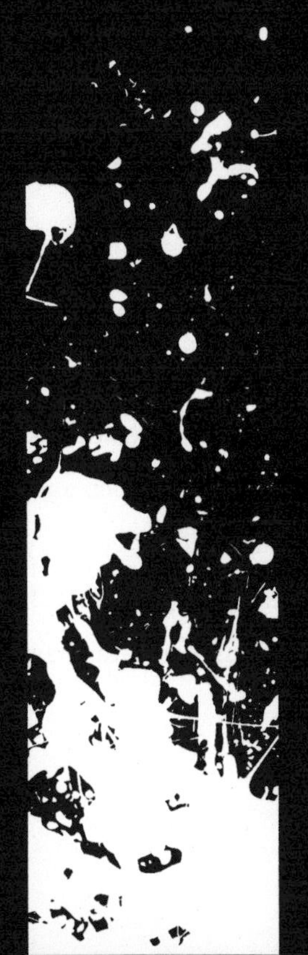

We push on, Dr. Cerveris calling the shots, leading the way. I ask Reilly about Mr. Burke, if he's safe. Reilly says he doesn't think my ex-teacher is in the complex at the moment, though he can't be sure. I start to ask Dr. Cerveris, but then he stops at another door and tells Reilly to open it.

Rage steps out, cool as you like. He raises an eyebrow at us and grins. "Are we going on a picnic?"

"This is no time for levity," Dr. Cerveris snaps. "The complex has come under attack from an unidentified enemy."

"I heard," Rage nods. "There was all sorts of fighting going on outside my door. I was confused at first. Then I figured it out." He cracks his knuckles. "How bad are things, sir?"

"Critical," Dr. Cerveris mutters. "The complex has been overrun. Our forces will regain control eventually, even if extra troops have to be summoned, but I have no confidence that stability will be resumed anytime soon. Our lives are in very real danger."

"Do we have a plan?" Rage asks as we jog on, only Danny left to gather.

"Once we're all together, we'll lock ourselves into a secure room and wait."

"That's all you've come up with?" Rage asks Reilly, chuckling bleakly.

"Just be glad we came for you," Reilly snaps. "We could have left you to rot."

"Oh, I am glad, sir, truly," Rage says. Then, to my astonishment, he slams an elbow into Reilly's nose, dropping the soldier to the floor. As Reilly slumps with a muffled yelp, Rage grabs the soldier's gun and takes it from him.

"What the hell are you–" Dr. Cerveris starts to roar.

Rage turns and jabs a finger into the doctor's eye, popping it as easily as he would a grape. As the scientist screams, Rage sucks on his finger. "Yummy," he grins. Then his face goes hard and he drives his hand through the side of Dr. Cerveris's skull, cracks it open and scoops out a handful of brain.

My field of vision narrows when I spot the fresh chunks of brain. Pain shoots through me, but it's a pleasurable pain. My mouth falls open and I advance, the other zom heads shuffling with me, all of us focused on the juicy substance in Rage's hand.

"Nuh-uh," Rage jeers, and thrusts the fistful of brain into his mouth. He chews with relish and kicks back Peder as he darts towards the one-eyed doctor. "He's all mine," Rage barks, and swiftly shovels out more of the dead man's brain.

I feel disappointment and start to turn away, looking for a victim of my own. Then my senses click back into place and I shake my head.

"What have you done?" I roar, startling the others. They lose their vacant look.

Rage is smirking. "A growing boy needs his vittles, that's what my gran used to say."

He drops the carcass of Dr. Cerveris and smiles tightly at Reilly, who is back on his feet and staring at Rage with unconcealed terror. "No need to brick it, Reilly. I'm not going to eat you. I've had my fill for the day."

"Why did you kill him?" Cathy groans, staring, nauseated, at the motionless scientist. "He was trying to help us."

"So that he could experiment on us some more?" Rage huffs. "Screw that."

"But you were always their favorite," Tiberius notes. "You did everything they asked. Their golden boy."

"Yeah," Rage says. "And they fell for it." He savagely kicks the

corpse of Dr. Cerveris. "I've hated these bastards since day one. No one locks *me* up like a lab rat and gets away with it. But there was no point hitting out at them when they had the upper hand. So I waited. I had a feeling something like this would happen, that things would break down and an opportunity would present itself. I didn't think it'd be as spectacular as this, but I was sure there'd be a bit of give somewhere along the line."

Rage looks at Reilly and cocks his head. "You still here?"

"I didn't think I was free to go," Reilly says shakily.

"Well, you are." Rage shrugs. "You weren't the worst of them. That doesn't mean I won't kill you if I have to, but at the moment you're not a threat to me, so be a sensible boy and bugger off."

"What about my gun?" Reilly asks.

"Do I look like an idiot?" Rage snorts. "You'd put a bullet through my skull the second I gave it back to you. I'm sure you'll pick up something in one of the ammo rooms. If you make it that far."

Reilly looks at the rest of us for support, but nobody says anything. "Fine," he grunts. "Damn you all too."

He takes off at top speed, desperately searching for something to defend himself with.

I focus on Rage and the gun in his hand. Rage stares back at me, then casts his gaze over the other zom heads. For a moment I think he's going to drop us all. But then he lowers the gun and smiles. "I would say it's been fun and that I'm going to miss you, but I'd be lying through my teeth."

He turns to leave.

"Where are you going?" Cathy cries.

"This way," Rage says, then points in the opposite direction. "If you follow me, I'll kill you, so I'd suggest you go that way."

"What about Danny?" Mark asks. "We haven't rescued him yet."

"Screw him," Rage says.

"You can't go off by yourself," Gokhan protests. "It's dangerous here, innit? We should stick together."

"Stick with you bunch of losers?" Rage laughs. "No way. So long, suckers!"

Then he flips us the finger and is gone.

NINETEEN

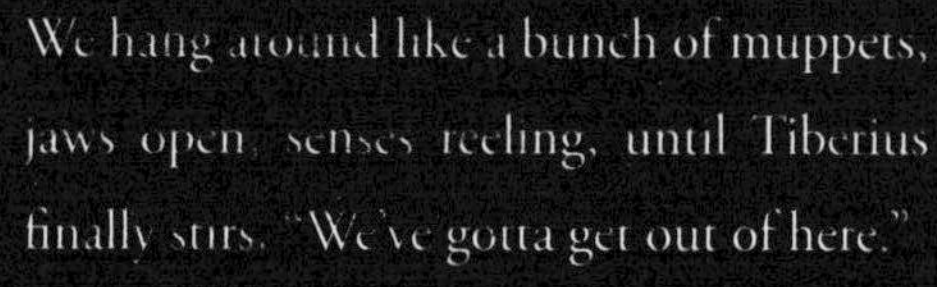

We hang around like a bunch of muppets, jaws open, senses reeling, until Tiberius finally stirs. "We've gotta get out of here."

"What about Danny?" Mark asks.

"Do you have any idea where his cell is?" Tiberius replies.

"No."

"Then forget about him."

"Wait a moment." I can't believe what I'm thinking as I stare at the remains of Dr. Cerveris.

"You want to tuck into his brain?" Cathy sneers. "Good luck — I doubt Rage left much."

"It's not that — although now that you mention it . . ."

Scraps of brain dot the interior of the dead doctor's head. Ignoring my feelings

of disgust, I run my fingers around it, then suck them, drawing a small burst of strength from the meager blobs. When the rest of the zom heads see that, they push in and copy me. They all come away with flecks of brain on their fingers, though I got the lion's share of what was left.

When we've scraped Dr. Cerveris's skull completely clean, I return to it, stick a hand into the hole in the doctor's head, then feel around until I find the back of the eye that Rage didn't puncture. I push softly while cutting around the flesh at the front of the socket with my other hand.

"What's she doing?" Cathy squeals. "Has she gone mad?"

"I don't think so," Tiberius mutters. "The sensors... If we want to get out of here, we'll have to get through doors that require fingerprints and a retinal scan."

Dr. Cerveris's eye oozes from its socket. I wipe the goo away, cup it gently in my palm and step back. "I did the eye. Who's gonna cut off one of his hands?"

There's a pause. Then Gokhan bends and starts slicing.

"This is *so* gross," Cathy moans, but her lips are twitching and I can tell she's trying hard not to smile. I feel like chuckling too. It shouldn't be funny, but it is. I'm sure I'll feel awful later when I look back on this, but right now I'm on an unnatural high.

"Nice of him to lend us a hand," Tiberius deadpans, and I almost explode with laughter. I'm not the only one.

"Come on," Mark snaps. He doesn't find this in any way entertaining. "If we're to escape, we'll need to be quick, before they find us."

"Who are *they*, Worm?" Peder snorts.

"The soldiers or the people who attacked." Mark shrugs. "One's as bad as the other, right?"

"What if they're here to free us?" Cathy says. "Maybe it's an army of zom heads come to break us out."

I remember Mr. Dowling and the spiders. "No," I sigh. "I don't know who or what they are, but they haven't come to help us. Mark's right. We need to split ASAP, before we end up like Dr. Cerveris."

I start off in the direction that Rage sent us, not wanting to risk a run-in with him, and after a moment of hesitation the rest of them fall in behind me.

I think about the butchered Dr. Cerveris as we progress, worrying about what happened. It wasn't the fact that Rage killed him that bugs me. It's how I reacted. I was on the verge of losing control. The sight of the brain triggered something inside me, and I almost switched off and went into full-on zombie mode.

I would have eaten anybody's brain right then. If I hadn't recovered my wits by chance, I'd have gone after Reilly. If I'd killed him and feasted, that would have been the end of me. I know that fresh brains are essential for revitalizeds, that I need to eat to hold on to my senses. But if I'd given in to my baser instincts and fed in such a grisly, inhuman fashion, I think I would have regressed anyway, and gladly, all too happy to leave my conscious self behind.

I'm clinging onto my semi-humanity, but only just. It won't be long now. Soon I'll hit a critical point and then it's bye-bye, Becky Smith, *hellooooo*, zom-B!

TWENTY

We flee without any real plan in mind. I ask the others, as we run, if they have an idea of the layout of the complex, if they've seen more of it than I have. They all reply negatively. Mark has been to a lab that the rest of us haven't visited, but it wasn't far from zom HQ.

"I've always assumed we were underground," Tiberius says, "because of the lack of daylight. But that's not necessarily the case. We might simply be in the middle of a huge building."

"No," Peder says. "I once heard a soldier grumbling about being stuck down here. Reilly told him to shut up—I don't think they were supposed to mention anything about where we are—but it was too late."

"Then I guess we need to head for the top," I grunt. "Let's look for stairs."

We push open every door that we pass and peer through every window. In the dark glass of one pane I catch sight of my reflection and pause. There's a small red *z* on my right cheek. I frown, wondering how it got there. Then I recall the clown stroking my face. Shivering, I wipe the mark from my flesh and hurry on.

"Here!" Cathy shouts. She's looking through a round panel of glass in a door. I press up beside her and spot a flight of stairs. I shake the door but it's locked. There's a control panel beside it.

"Time to test our toys," I grin tightly. "Gokhan, you first. They usually press their fingers to the sensor before scanning their eye."

Gokhan holds Dr. Cerveris's fingers up to the panel. There's a small beeping noise. I open my hand and reveal the eye. I roll it in my palm until it's pointing the right way, then rest it in front of the retinal scanner. I have no confidence that it will work now that it's been ripped from its socket, but to my delight there's a second beep and the door slides open.

"Eye, eye!" Tiberius snickers, slipping past me and jogging up the stairs.

It's only a single flight of steps. Seconds later we're on a higher floor, identical to the one below, so we go looking for an exit or the next set of stairs. There are zombies loose on this level too, but they don't interfere with us. They shoot us dark looks and sniff the air

hungrily when they catch our scent, but when they realize we're not walking snack boxes, they leave us be.

We find another set of stairs and climb, this time up three levels. Once again we search for a way out. But after a couple of minutes Mark looks through an open door and does a double take. "What the hell...?" he mutters.

"Worm!" Cathy barks. "This is no time for—"

"Shh!" he snaps, and the look on his face tells us this is serious.

Curious, we crowd around Mark and gape, slack jawed, at the hellish drama unfurling within.

It's a massive room, the largest I've seen in the complex. Judging by the TV sets hanging from the walls, I'm guessing it's a relaxation area, a much grander version of zom HQ.

Quite a lot of the staff are here, shoved up against one of the walls. They're surrounded by snapping, howling zombies. But the living dead are only occasionally attacking. They're being held in check by a team of people in hoodies. The zombie masters have wrinkled flesh, an ugly mass of purple patches and pustulant, peeling skin. They have pale yellow eyes, and if their hoodies slipped I know we'd see crops of unhealthy gray hair. I also know that they have no fingernails and their tongues are scabby and shriveled.

They're the mutants I saw in my school, and before that on a visit to the Imperial War Museum. They were controlling zombies the last time I saw them, and they're in command now too, directing the reviveds with blasts of the whistles that hang on strings from the neck of each mutant.

In the middle of the mutants and zombies is the clown, Mr. Dowling. He towers above the rest of them, which is strange, as I didn't think he was unusually tall when I saw him in my cell. Glancing down, I see that he's on stilts, balanced elegantly.

Mr. Dowling is waving his hands above his head, swaying gently, beaming insanely.

"Come on," one of the mutants croaks at the weeping, moaning humans huddled against the wall. "Sing or we'll set the doggies on you again. *Sing!*"

The other mutants take up the refrain and start to bellow, "Sing! Sing! Sing!"

Mr. Dowling giggles shrilly and twirls his arms like an orchestra conductor. The soldiers, scientists and nurses begin to chant together, having obviously been told what to sing before we hit the scene. They're out of tune, and not all in sync, but the song is unmistakable.

"Jingle bells, jingle bells,
Jingle all the way,
Oh what fun it is to ride
In a one-horse open sleigh."

The mutants screech with delight and clap enthusiastically. Mr. Dowling sighs happily and cups his hands to his heart, then wipes a finger across his cheeks as if to remove tears of joy. A couple of zombies dart forward and drag humans from the crowd. They carve their skulls open and tuck in. The survivors sing another creepy chorus of "Jingle Bells" at the rough prompting of the mutants.

While the doomed humans are singing, Mr. Dowling points at a woman and beckons her forward. She shakes her head, terrified, tears coursing down her cheeks. The clown frowns, then draws a finger across his throat. One of the mutants blows his whistle and a zombie drags the woman out and tears into her.

Mr. Dowling smiles and points to another woman. This one hurries forward, not even waiting for him to beckon. When she's in front of him, his smile widens and he bends over and opens his lips. I expect a stream of spiders to come spilling out, but this time he reaches into his mouth and pulls out a scorpion. It's alive and twisting wildly in his grip.

The clown puts a finger to the woman's lips and taps them. With a gulp, she opens her mouth. He sticks his tongue out, then nods at her to do the same. With a delirious giggle, he lays the scorpion on her tongue, then nods for her to close her mouth. With fresh tears, she obeys his command, then falls away a moment later, coughing and choking.

The mutants cackle and kick the woman. The zombies hiss and a few more dart into the fray and emerge clutching struggling, screaming humans.

Then Mr. Dowling's head turns and he trains his gaze on us. No... not on us... on *me*.

There's no doubt in my mind that he's looking at me specifically. His eyes burn into mine and his lips twitch as if he's just spotted a dear friend. When the mutants see us, they squeal and dart towards us, dragging zombies with them.

Mr. Dowling makes a high whining noise and they stop instantly. As they retreat, he extends a hand towards me, turns it upside down, then slowly crooks his middle finger, beckoning me forward.

"Not even in your sodding dreams!" I scream, then whirl and race away, not caring if the others follow, not worrying about the direction I'm taking, knowing only that I have to get far away from the clown as quickly as possible, before he takes me into his embrace and turns me into something even worse than one of the walking, undead damned.

TWENTY-ONE

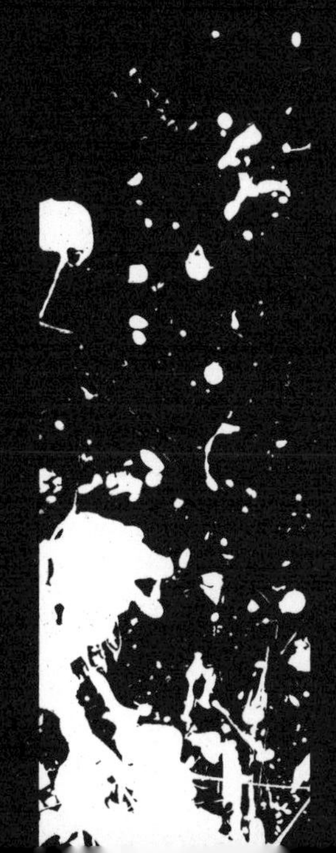

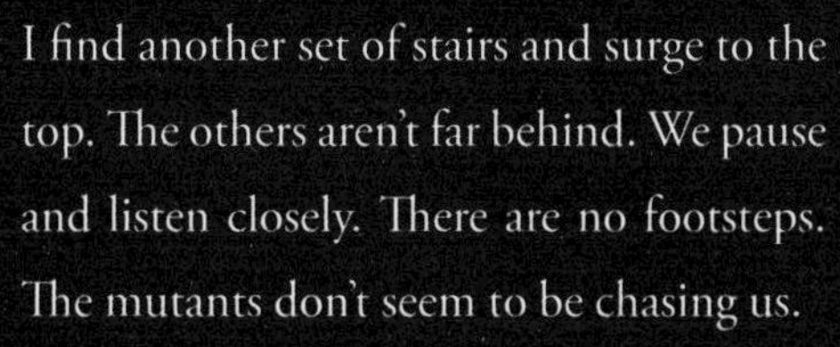

I find another set of stairs and surge to the top. The others aren't far behind. We pause and listen closely. There are no footsteps. The mutants don't seem to be chasing us.

I double over and make a sighing sound. I feel like I should be panting, but of course I can't, since my lungs don't work properly.

"Who the hell was that guy in the clown outfit?" Cathy moans.

"And those freaks in the hoodies," Peder exclaims. "Were they zombies? Humans? What?"

"I don't think they're either," I tell him. "They're mutants. They were there when my school was invaded. It looks like they work for Mr. Dowling – the clown – but I've no idea what he is, or why they're here, or why the zombies obey them, or..." I shake my head and scowl. "They don't matter. We need to get out of here. We can wonder about it later."

"But what if they come after us?" Cathy whimpers.

"All the more reason to get a move on," Tiberius grunts, and off we set again.

Time seems to slow as we search for another set of stairs. We can't find any, and the longer we go on, the more our spirits dip. We're all in rough shape. The bits of brain we sucked from Dr. Cerveris's head didn't do much for us. The shooting pains are coming regularly now and I know the others are feeling them too by the way they wince and twitch every few minutes. My thoughts are starting to swim. It's getting harder to focus.

"I think we've come the wrong way," Gokhan mutters. "Just because we're underground, it don't mean the exit has to be at the top, eh? Maybe it's at the bottom, a tunnel that leads to an elevator or something."

Peder frowns. "But if we head down and don't find it, what then?"

"We come back up," Gokhan says.

"That means slipping past the clown and his mutants a couple of times," Peder growls. "I don't fancy that."

"Maybe we don't have to," Cathy says. "There must be other flights of stairs. We've been taking the first set that we've found on every floor. Let's go down a level and–"

"Wait," Mark mutters, looking at the ceiling. "Did any of you have attic stairs at home, the sort that rest inside the attic when you're not using them?"

"What sort of a question is that?" Cathy sneers.

"My parents put in a set a few years ago," Mark says stiffly, ignoring her. "If you have steps like that, you use a thin pole to open the door, which is part of the stairs. In our home, the hole you stuck the tip of the pole into looked just like that one up there."

I squint and spot the small opening that he's talking about. "So there's an attic. So what?"

"Why would they have an attic in an underground building?" Mark asks softly.

I stare harder at the hole. "You think it's something else?"

"It has to be." He shrugs. "I mean, it might just be a machine room or housing for an air-conditioning unit. But wouldn't they have signs up if that was the case, like they have elsewhere?"

"I haven't noticed any signs," Peder grunts.

"Then you haven't been paying as much attention as me," Mark says smugly, then starts looking for a pole. We search too and a minute later we find one in a nearby room, tucked away in a corner.

I try to unlock the attic door but my hands are trembling and I can't guide in the narrow tip. Peder and Tiberius try too, but both fail, their hands shaking as badly as mine.

"Give it to me," Mark snaps, losing patience, and slots it in at the first attempt. His hands are remarkably steady. He doesn't seem to be suffering like the rest of us. Maybe the doctors slipped him some nutrients on the sly when they were operating on him.

A set of steps drops smoothly as the door opens. I feel a stab of excitement. But before I can head up, Cathy pushes me aside and I stumble and fall over. "Ladies first," she chuckles.

I scowl as she trots up, Peder, Gokhan and Tiberius just behind her. Mark helps me to my feet. "Are you okay?" he asks.

"Sure. But I'm gonna give her a thumping when this is–"

Two soldiers and a female scientist spill into the corridor. The scientist is babbling, "...right here. The pole's in a room. Once we open the door, we can..." She spots Mark and me and curses.

One of the soldiers has a gun. He aims quickly and fires. A bullet rips by my head but misses.

"Up the steps!" I roar at Mark.

The soldier fires again, three times. One of the bullets strikes Mark's left arm and blood sprays from it. He cries out and whirls away from the stairs. I duck as the soldier fires again, grab Mark and hurl him at the steps. He scrambles up them. I'm about to start after him, then pause, pick up the pole and throw it up into the space ahead of me.

A bullet hits the flesh on my back where my heart used to be. If I was whole, it would open up a nasty wound. But because I'm more hole than whole in that part of my body, it only nicks a flap of skin and shoots on through the cavity and out the other side.

I hurry after Mark and pull the steps up behind me, locking them into place. The humans scream beneath us and the soldier fires a stream of bullets into the ceiling, either trying to hit us or smash the lock. I don't hang around to find out. Pushing Mark ahead of me, I scurry after the others.

We're in a corridor, not an attic, lit dimly by soft red lights. The dimness is a relief after the brightness of the complex. I hadn't realized how much the glare of the lights hurt.

We shuffle along, nobody saying anything. The corridor angles upwards, then turns back on itself and keeps rising. The noises of the complex fade the farther on we push. I feel real hope for the first time. The nurse was leading the soldiers to this place and seemed desperate to reach it. Because it's a way out? Not the main exit, but a secret escape route for those of a certain rank?

The corridor snakes around several times before the floor levels out and we step through into a large, square room. There are doorways in the middle of all four walls. Two are open, like ours, leading to corridors like the one we've stepped out of. A metal door stands in the fourth. It's like no other door that we've seen in the complex, taller, wider, more impressive.

"That must be it!" Peder whoops, racing towards the door.

"The exit!" Cathy gasps, then spins towards me. "Do you still have the eye? You didn't drop it, did you? Tell me you didn't–"

I hold up my hand and widen my fingers, letting her see the eye.

"Yes!" she shouts.

I grin and push past, giving her a sharp dig with my elbow to pay her back for pushing me aside earlier. Cathy doesn't care. She only has eyes for the door.

Gokhan presses Dr. Cerveris's fingers to the panel and it beeps. Tiberius and Peder shut their mouths as if to hold their breath, both forgetting that they can't actually breathe.

I step forward and hold up the eye. A camera scans it. There's an agonizing pause in which I convince myself that it isn't going to work, that I've shaken the eye around too much, dislodged something vital inside. Then...

Beep.

Everyone cheers as if I'd just scored the winning goal in a cup final.

The cheers stop when the system beeps again and a touch-screen calculator flashes up on the panel where Gokhan scanned in the dead doctor's fingerprints. There's a short message just below it.

Please enter six-digit authorization code.

We stare at the message, then at each other.

I clear my throat. "This is where someone says that they're a hacker and they can crack this bastard in five minutes flat."

Nobody says a word.

"Damn," I sigh, sinking to my haunches. "In that case I guess we just rot here and turn into rabid, brain-munching reviveds."

TWENTY-TWO

Tiberius starts keying in random numbers. Every time he completes a string of six figures, the screen beeps and clears itself, prompting him to try again.

"It's pointless," Mark says glumly. "There's no way you're going to key in the exact six numbers by accident."

"Shut up," Tiberius snarls, staying focused on the screen. "Maybe it's a simple code, six zeros or nines, just to stop any zombies from getting through."

Mark makes a face but says nothing. He sits beside me and tugs at the material around the wound left by the bullet. Blood is oozing out of the hole. The smell of it tickles my nostrils, and for some reason I find myself licking my lips.

I look more closely and realize Mark's

blood is different than mine. It's not congealed. It doesn't stop flowing within a couple of seconds. It's red and pure, just like...

"What's that smell?" Gokhan asks, crinkling his nose.

"Me," I say too loudly, lurching to my feet and tugging at the flesh around the hole where my heart should be. "I was shot. I'm bleeding. It'll pass in a–"

"No," Gokhan silences me. "This is different, innit? It smells like human blood. But it can't be. We're alone. Where's it coming from, eh?"

The others are sniffing the air too, even Tiberius, who isn't looking at the screen anymore. I try to think of a way to distract them before they make the same logical leap that I have. Before I can, Peder shushes everyone.

"Quiet," he snaps. "I can hear something."

"Don't be stupid," I tell him. "You're imagining things. It's just–"

"Shut the hell up!" he roars, then squints suspiciously. "That noise... it's like a drumbeat, only softer...."

It's silent in this room. Not like anywhere else in the complex, where there was always the rumbling thunder of machinery to contend with. You wouldn't hear a pin drop, but you can hear a lot of soft sounds that were masked in zom HQ and the corridors, especially if your ears are as sharp as ours. Noises like a gentle burp, a soft sneeze, someone's stomach rumbling.

Or a heartbeat.

The zom heads start to turn, nostrils flaring, eyes glassy, ears cocked, locking in on the source of the smell and noise. I shuffle my feet to distract them and start to tell them again that they're imagining things, terrified of what will happen when they figure it out.

"There!" Cathy yells, leaping across the room. I try to stop her but she bowls me aside, the excitement of the discovery lending her an extra burst of strength. Mark gapes at her as she shoves him back against the wall.

"What the hell are you doing?" he roars as she hooks her finger bones into the bandages around his chest and stomach, the fabric of his clothes, the padded vest beneath. I scramble after her but Peder grabs the back of my neck and forces me down. His eyes are bright and he's staring fixedly at Cathy.

"Leave me alone," Mark yelps, struggling feebly. "Get off of me, you nutcase. You'll expose my burns."

Cathy ignores him and keeps on ripping. Tiberius starts to close in, eyes like a shark's, lips pulling back over his teeth, fingers opening and closing.

"Please!" Mark shrieks, starting to panic now. "The doctors said I'd fall apart if I didn't stay wrapped up. Please, Cathy, don't do this. Please!"

Cathy ignores him and slices through the last of the covering. Mark clutches for the bandages as they fall away and reveal his flesh. Then he catches sight of himself and stops, frowning, one step behind everybody else.

"I don't understand," he whispers, poking at his stomach with a gloved finger. His skin is pale from being under wraps for so long, but there are no burn marks. His flesh is pure.

"Your gloves," Peder says in a choked voice, pushing himself off me, transfixed by the sight of Mark's flesh. "Take them off."

Mark frowns, then tugs at the glove covering his left hand. It doesn't detach. As he continues pulling at it, Cathy loses patience, takes hold and rips it away. Mark shouts with pain, then stares with shock. There are bits of metal attached to the ends of his fingers.

"What's happening?" Mark croaks. "I don't understand."

But this time it's a lie. The tumblers have clicked for him at last. Even without the exposed flesh, the fake finger bones, the rise and fall of his stomach as he breathes, the soft sound of his heart as it beats, he could tell by the fixed, frenzied looks in the eyes of the zom heads around him.

"Mark's alive," Cathy whispers.

Then licks her lips.

Hungry.

TWENTY-THREE

"No," Mark wheezes. "This can't be right. I'm a zom head. I was attacked. I was killed. There's been a mistake."

The zombies – and that's what they are now, all human semblance discarded – don't reply. They're shuffling closer, eyes steady, ready to feed.

"Get back," I snarl, leaping to my feet and pushing Cathy away. I step between Mark and the others. "You're not going to do this. I'm hungry too. I can smell him just like you can, and it's driving me wild. But I won't harm him and I won't let you lot either. You have to control yourselves. This is *Mark*."

"Worm," Cathy gurgles, grinning crookedly. "Wriggle, little worm."

"No!" I roar, slamming my hands together, trying to startle them back to their senses. "Stop. Think. Don't give in to the hunger. Peder. Gokhan. Tiberius." I turn pleadingly to the ginger-haired teenager. "You stood by my side. You fought for my life. Do the same for Mark. You have to. He's one of us." A memory clicks in. *"We accept him! Gooble gobble!"*

Tiberius pauses and his eyes clear slightly.

"It must have been an experiment," I babble. "They wanted to see if they could hide a human among us. They told him he was a zombie. They covered him up so that we couldn't smell him, hear his heartbeat or see him breathing. They must have given him drugs to keep his eyes open, dry out his mouth, stop him from sweating, make him look like he was a revitalized."

"But he's not," Peder growls. "He's human."

"I didn't know," Mark wails. "I thought...they told me...I never even guessed! B, you've got to stop them. Don't let them eat me. Please, B, I want to live, I don't want to–"

"Shh. I'm trying." I concentrate on Tiberius, hoping that if I can reach him, he can help me get through to the rest of them. "All right, he's not a proper zom head, but he's still one of us. He's been living alongside you guys for months. You can't turn on him as if he doesn't mean anything to you."

"Worm," Cathy leers again, reaching out for the trembling boy.

I slap her hands away. "I know you don't respect him, you bully him, you treat him like a worm. But he's still part of the gang. You won't attack one of your own. You're not monsters. It's the hunger. You have to fight it. You–"

Gokhan smashes a fist into my jaw and I stagger sideways. Mark shrieks and the sound excites them. They press forward. Before they can target him, I'm back between them, punching and kicking, screaming abusively. I'm not going to accept this. I let Tyler Bayor die. I won't let it happen to Mark too.

"Stop!" I yell. "You don't know what you're doing!"

Peder grabs the neck of my T-shirt and pulls me in close. His eyes flash as he grins at me. "Yes we do," he hisses.

"Tiberius!" I bellow. "Help me! We have to fight together! You have to–"

Tiberius puts a finger to my lips and says, "Hush now." Then he grabs me from Peder and throws me aside.

Mark screams. "No! God! Help!"

But not even God can help him now.

The zombies fall on the boy. They dig their fingers into his skull and tear it open. Ram claws into his brain and scoop it out. They ignore his screams, his whimpers, his pleas, the feeble thrashing of his arms and legs.

And all I can do as the beasts feast and Mark dies wretchedly before my eyes, calling my name, begging for mercy, is beat the floor uselessly with my fists and howl insanely at the cruel injustices of this monstrous, twisted world.

TWENTY-FOUR

"What have you done?"

I'm backed up against the wall close to the sealed door. My finger bones are digging into the concrete, tearing at the plaster. I stare with shock and disgust at the zom heads as they squat close to Mark's remains, licking their fingers clean, dipping them back inside his emptied skull in search of any last tidbits. They look happy, sated, *full*. They pay no attention to me. Like junkies after a fix. Spaced out. In a world of their own. A world of murder, cannibalism and sweet, sweet brains.

"Oh, God, what have you sick bastards *done*?" I moan, shaking my head, trying to close my eyes to the nightmare, praying for tears that will never come.

Tiberius glances at me and frowns. He

gazes at Mark, then at his fingers. For a moment he looks like himself and he cringes. A look of regret and terror flickers across his face. Then his jaw tightens and I see him turn away from remorse. He gives himself over to the pleasure of the feed and zones out again.

Cathy is giggling. She pokes out one of Mark's eyes, the way I poked out Dr. Cerveris's earlier, and plays with it. She puts it in her mouth, sucks on it a while, then spits it up into the air and tries to catch it with her tongue as it drops. She misses. It hits her chin and bounces away. She giggles again.

Peder and Gokhan are still fishing for scraps of brain. Gokhan is muttering, "Innit. Innit. Innit." Peder nudges him aside, crouches over Mark like a dog and sticks his face into the cavity of the dead boy's head to lick out any last morsels.

"You're monsters," I sob. But they're not really. They're just hungry creatures who fed when prey was presented to them. I identify with the zom heads too closely to condemn them completely. I had to fight hard not to turn on Mark. If it had been five minutes later, or ten or thirty or however long I have left before my senses crumble, I would have joined in.

I could be harsh and say that they haven't regressed, they're still revitalizeds, they had a choice. But who am I to judge? I was able to fight temptation because I can naturally hold out longer or because I ate slightly more of Dr. Cerveris's brain than they did. Maybe they weren't able to resist the way I was.

Either way, I'm sure they'll feel guilty later, once the feeding frenzy passes and they recover their wits. They'll probably spend the rest of their conscious days regretting the way they gave in to their base instincts. That won't do poor Mark any good, but at least they'll suffer. I think they'll probably envy me once I lose my grip and regress. The only way they're ever going to escape the awful memory of their crime is by shedding their humanity entirely and becoming dumb reviveds again.

As I pause between moans, I hear a noise in one of the corridors. Footsteps. I tear my gaze away from the vile spectacle and watch sluggishly as Josh Massoglia enters the room, a small team of soldiers spreading out to flank him.

Two of the soldiers are carrying flamethrowers.

The zom heads pay no attention to the soldiers. Mark's brain was enough for them. They don't need any more at the moment. They don't even react when the pair with flamethrowers takes aim.

"Wait," Josh says. He's staring at me. My fingers are still scratching the wall. My head is shaking softly.

Josh crosses the room and stops in front of me. He looks at my fingers, my lips, then into my eyes. His right hand comes up slowly and stretches out towards the calculator on the screen. He keys in six numbers and it makes a beeping sound.

The door slides open.

Josh steps away from me and lowers his hand. He doesn't say anything. My fingers fall still. My head turns towards the open door. Bewildered, I look to Josh for confirmation, but he doesn't give me any signs.

I peel myself away from the wall and stumble through the doorway, into a corridor that rises like the one I was in before. I feel as if I'm in a dream, but I can't be. The dead don't sleep, so the dead can't dream.

The door starts to slide shut behind me. I step to the side, looking for Josh one last time, searching for answers. But all I see is a sudden blossoming of red and yellow flames.

There are agonized screams, the voices of four teenagers blending into one as the zom heads pay the ultimate price for turning on Mark. The stench of burning flesh, flames consuming all, both the monsters and their victim.

Then the door clicks shut and there's nothing.

Only me.

My cheeks are dry but I wipe a hand across them anyway, brushing away nonexistent tears. Then I turn and stagger up the corridor. I expect it to twist back on itself like the other one did, but this just keeps rising until it levels out into a tiny room. There's a plain wooden door in one of the walls, no scanners, locks or anything. I can smell the outside world, a rich, pungent, overwhelming scent after the clinical, carefully maintained atmosphere of the complex.

With a moan born more of confused dread than delight, I shuffle forward, push open the door, leave the nightmarish gloom of the underground behind me and step out into sunlight.

To be continued...